Savannah Spectator Blind Item

Dear Readers,

The Savannah summer nights have surely been heating up passions! Case in point: a prodigal son of our most famous family has returned from the wilds of his Wyoming ranch to attend his uncle's senatorial bid fund-raiser. But he didn't come alone. He came with his young son, and the boy's nanny. A young gorgeous nanny with curves in all the right places to get any cowboy's blood pumping. No demure governess she—not while wearing a backless dress that had half of Savannah's gentlemen drooling at the sight!

Alas our cowboy and his nanny spent an all-too-brief time in Savannah. What awaits them in Wyoming? Passion, sex, a horseback ride into the sunset? Or merely hay fever, dust and cow patties? As soon as this reporter knows, you can bet *you'll* know!

D0802140

Dear Reader,

Yes, we have what you're looking for at Silhouette Desire. This month, we bring you some of the most anticipated stories…and some of the most exciting new tales we have ever offered.

Yes, *New York Times* bestselling author Lisa Jackson is back with Randi McCafferty's story. You've been waiting to discover who fathered Randi's baby and who was out to kill her, and the incomparable Lisa Jackson answers all your questions and more in *Best-Kept Lies*. Yes, we have the next installment of DYNASTIES: THE DANFORTHS with Cathleen Galitz's *Cowboy Crescendo*. And you can be sure that wild Wyoming rancher Toby Danforth is just as hot as can be. Yes, there is finally another SECRETS! book from Barbara McCauley. She's back with *Miss Pruitt's Private Life*, a scandalous tale of passionate encounters and returning characters you've come to know and love.

Yes, Sara Orwig continues her compelling series STALLION PASS: TEXAS KNIGHTS with an outstanding tale of stranded strangers turned secret lovers, in *Standing Outside the Fire*. Yes, the fabulous Kathie DeNosky is back this month with a scintillating story about a woman desperate to have a *Baby at His Convenience*. And yes, Bronwyn Jameson is taking us down under as two passionate individuals square off in a battle that soon sweeps them *Beyond Control*.

Here's hoping you'll be saying "Yes, yes, yes" to Silhouette Desire all month…all summer…all year long!

Melissa Jeglinski

Melissa Jeglinski
Senior Editor
Silhouette Desire

Please address questions and book requests to:
Silhouette Reader Service
U.S.: 3010 Walden Ave., P.O. Box 1325, Buffalo, NY 14269
Canadian: P.O. Box 609, Fort Erie, Ont. L2A 5X3

DYNASTIES: THE DANFORTHS

COWBOY CRESCENDO
CATHLEEN GALITZ

Published by Silhouette Books
America's Publisher of Contemporary Romance

Special thanks and acknowledgment are given to Cathleen Galitz for her contribution to the DYNASTIES: THE DANFORTHS series.

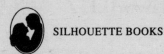 SILHOUETTE BOOKS

ISBN 0-373-76591-6

COWBOY CRESCENDO

Books by Cathleen Galitz

Silhouette Desire

The Cowboy Takes a Bride #1271
Wyoming Cinderella #1373
Her Boss's Baby #1396
Tall, Dark...and Framed? #1433
Warrior in Her Bed #1506
Pretending with the Playboy #1569
Cowboy Crescendo #1591

Silhouette Romance

The Cowboy Who Broke the Mold #1257
100% Pure Cowboy #1279
Wyoming Born & Bred #1381

CATHLEEN GALITZ,

a Wyoming native, teaches English to students in grades six through twelve in a rural school that houses kinder-gartners and seniors in the same building. She feels blessed to have married a man who is both supportive and patient. When she's not busy writing, teaching or chauf-feuring her sons to and from various activities, she can most likely be found indulging in her favorite pastime— reading.

DYNASTIES: THE DANFORTHS

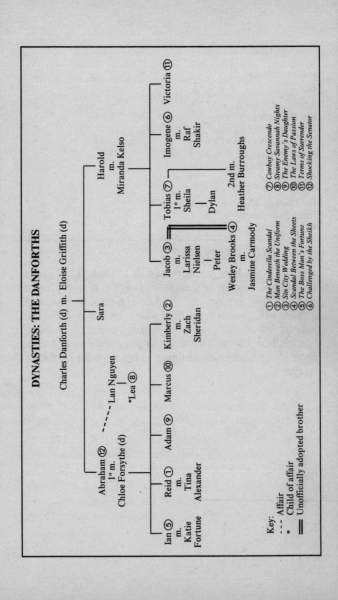

Charles Danforth (d) m. Eloise Griffith (d)

Sara

Harold
m.
Miranda Kelso

Abraham ⑫
1st m.
Chloe Forsythe (d)

Lan Nguyen
|
*Lea ⑧

Ian ⑤
m.
Katie
Fortune

Reid ①
m.
Tina
Alexander

Adam ⑨

Marcus ⑩

Kimberly ②
m.
Zach
Sheridan

Jacob ③
m.
Larissa
Nielsen
|
Peter

Wesley Brooks ④
m.
Jasmine Carmody

Tobias ⑦
1st m.
Sheila
|
Dylan

2nd m.
Heather Burroughs

Imogene ⑥
m.
Raf
Shakir

Victoria ⑪

① *The Cinderella Scandal*
② *Man Beneath the Uniform*
③ *Sin City Wedding*
④ *Scandal Between the Sheets*
⑤ *The Boss Man's Fortune*
⑥ *Challenged by the Sheikh*
⑦ *Cowboy Crescendo*
⑧ *Steamy Savannah Nights*
⑨ *The Enemy's Daughter*
⑩ *The Laws of Passion*
⑪ *Terms of Surrender*
⑫ *Shocking the Senator*

Key:
--- Affair
* Child of affair
═══ Unofficially adopted brother

One

Heather Burroughs stood in the doorway of her new employer's massive living room unable to believe what she was seeing.

Unable to stomach what she was hearing.

Since no one bothered answering her persistent attempts at making her presence at the front door known, she let herself in and followed the sound of a deep voice to the spot where she presently stood rooted in horror. Matching that voice to a particularly handsome face did little to allay Heather's fears that she had just been hired by a monster.

A monster who was presently taunting a child with a cookie.

"Say it, Dylan," the man coaxed, his voice straining with impatience.

He was so intent on imposing his will upon the toddler that he remained unaware of Heather's presence. A cherub of three reached out a chubby hand for the treat dangled in his face, only to have it snatched away the instant his fingers touched the sugary delight. Tears pooled in a pair of eyes the exact same color and shape as his tormenter's. It spilled down his ruddy cheeks and caused the monster to mumble a slight invective under his breath.

"Come on, Dylan. Just say it!"

Heather knew firsthand what it felt like to have a cookie dangled in front of one's face, and she wasn't about to stand idly by and watch her new employer play such mean-spirited games with his son—even if it did mean losing her job on the very first day of work.

Even if that job meant the difference between financial independence or possibly living on the streets.

"Give me that!"

Ignoring the man's startled look, Heather marched into the room and grabbed the cookie from his hands. She proceeded to bend down, wipe the tears from his little boy's face with the cuff of her sleeve and give him the cookie. Dylan accepted it with both hands and a look of pure gratitude, shoving as much of it into his mouth before his father could confiscate it. When he grinned up at Heather through a mouth-

gooey chocolate, it was all she could do to
from sweeping him up in her arms and making
break for the front door.

"Just who do you think you are, lady, and what
in the hell do you think you're doing?" Tobias Danforth demanded to know.

He glared at her from a squatting position on the
floor. The denim of his jeans was stretched taut over
thighs that strained as he rose to his full height of
six feet. He towered over Heather, who barely
weighed a hundred pounds soaking wet. In tennis
shoes, she was almost a foot shorter than he was.
She felt like David facing Goliath.

Without a slingshot.

Summoning her stage presence, Heather responded in a regal tone that belied the fact she was
the underling and he, technically, her boss.

"I'm the nanny the employment agency hired,
and what I'm doing is putting an end to you taunting
this boy. In case you're unaware of it, Mr. Danforth,
Dylan is a child, not an animal to be trained with
doggie biscuits."

"How dare you—"

"I dare because I care," she countered, sticking
her chin out as if daring him to take a shot at it.

Those icy-blue eyes of his pinned her to the spot
like some hapless butterfly in a child's science fair
project. Nonetheless, if this fellow thought he was
going to label Heather Burroughs a mere cowardus
interruptus, he had another thing coming. Having

endured the training of some of the most sadistic music teachers on the planet, it was going to take a whole lot more than an imposing presence to make her back down.

"And you think I don't care?"

His voice was sardonic.

And as cutting as the eyes trained on her.

What she beheld glimmering in those arctic depths was a ferocity that would send a wild wolf scurrying for protection. Placing her hands on her hips, she held her ground. Albeit on shaky legs.

"I doubt if Protective Services would approve of your type of parenting any more than I do," she told him, suddenly glad for the schooling that kept her voice from quavering in times of duress.

"Get out of my home, lady."

Though spoken so softly that the child caught between the two of them didn't so much as flinch, the man's words tore through Heather like bullets.

Why after twenty-five years of compliance she had finally discovered her backbone was as much a mystery to her as it was to her parents. They had all but disowned her for turning her back on their dreams. A neophyte at standing up for her beliefs, Heather had yet to develop the skills needed to temper her newfound assertiveness with prudence. The truth of the matter was that she was in no position to sacrifice this job unless she was ready to humble herself and, as her father had so bluntly put it, "come crawling back" to him for his support.

Still, she had no desire whatsoever to work for a man who struck her as being so very like her stern, demanding father. A man determined to withhold his approval unless his child performed up to his level of satisfaction.

Stiffening her spine, Heather started toward the door. She reminded herself that throughout the ages, scores of renowned musicians testified that poverty was good for the soul.

A tentative, childish voice stopped her in her tracks.

"Gookie!"

Tobias Danforth's face might as well have been made of wax the way his son's sudden outburst re-arranged his sharp, masculine features. Eyes that only a moment before had been as icy as a Wyoming lake in January thawed instantly. Dropping to his knees, he took the boy by both shoulders to peer into his eyes.

"What did you just say?"

Had his touch not been so overtly tender, Heather might well have jumped to the conclusion that he intended to shake a response out of the lad.

She wondered what kind of father couldn't understand his own child's adorable attempt at forming words. Because her throat had turned to dust, her own words sounded altogether too scratchy as she endeavored to enlighten the poor man.

"I believe he said *cookie*. For what it's worth, I think he'd like another one."

"For what it's worth, he can have the whole damn bag!" Tobias shouted in startling jubilation.

He grabbed Dylan up under the arms and swung him around in the air. The print of the boy's cowboy-themed shirt blurred into a brightly spinning top. The exuberant expression on his father's face caused Heather's pulse to skitter. It burst into a gallop before it came skidding to a dead stop. If it was possible that there might actually be a nice guy hiding behind the mask of a monster, she hoped he knew CPR.

Squealing with delight, Dylan repeated the feat that had earned him such an enthusiastic response.

"Gookie!"

That hard and judgmental something, lodged inside Heather's heart, softened to see unshed tears glistening in Tobias Danforth's eyes as he set his son down and ruffled his dark hair. The man was reputed to be worth millions and was looked upon by locals as somewhat of a reclusive mystery. Indeed, any outsider who could afford to treat ranching as a gentleman's hobby was generally regarded with suspicion among those born and bred of this unforgiving land. That such a man could actually be moved to tears by such an unremarkable accomplishment took Heather completely by surprise.

True to his word, Tobias grabbed the bag of cookies off a nearby ledge and handed it over to Dylan. Heather's dark suspicions about her former employer evaporated as the boy threw his arms around his daddy's neck and proceeded to cover his face with kisses. The scene was so unlike anything from her own childhood that Heather felt a pang of regret that her invitation to stick around long enough to get to know either of them better had been revoked.

As she turned to leave, she was halted by a Southern drawl as strong as a rope. And as tender as a prayer.

''And just where do you think you're going?''

Heather turned slowly around. The sight of her interrogator with chocolate-chip kisses smeared across his face did much to lessen the tension smoldering between them. The ghost of a smile made the angular planes of that face look far less formidable than the first impression Heather received of it.

''You just fired me,'' she reminded him gently.

Tobias took a clean white handkerchief out of his pocket and swiped at his face.

''Well, consider yourself un-fired.''

Heather's heart banged against her chest. If there was any chance of salvaging this job, she had better put a smile on her face and a conciliatory tone in her voice. Aside from the fact that she didn't want to be reduced to begging her parents for money, it would be almost impossible to find a position better suited to her needs at the present time. Not to mention she felt such an immediate connection with the child who was to be her charge. She reached out and took the handkerchief from Tobias's hand.

"Here, let me help you with that," she offered, dabbing at a crumb hanging from his mustache.

What was meant as a friendly gesture turned suddenly intimate as Tobias's eyes bored into hers. A shiver starting at the base of Heather's neck raced through her and played with every nerve ending in her body. A telltale tremble caused the handkerchief in her hand to resemble a white flag of surrender. As a general rule, Heather liked clean-shaven men, but as her gaze lingered upon the curve of the mouth peeking out from beneath a well-groomed mustache, she didn't think it would take much persuasion to change her mind.

Have you gone completely crazy? Heather asked herself.

She refused to fall into the same self-destructive pattern that had ruined the last relationship she'd had with a man, who had professed himself to be her mentor. She struggled to find something to say that would put their relationship back on professional footing. Entertaining romantic notions about an employer, no matter how handsome or baffling to the senses, was risking emotional suicide.

"We'd better discuss the terms of my employment before I accept your conditions—especially if they include the kind of behavior modification I saw you using on your son."

Tobias reached out to take her hand into his. Heather gasped at the intensity of the voltage that coursed through her body at his touch. The sound caused him to immediately release his grip. The handkerchief fluttered to the ground between them, a symbolic victim of the war between the sexes.

"Let me assure you, Miss Burroughs, I have no intention of compromising your virtue while you're in my employment, if that's what you're worried about. I can also wipe my own face, and my own butt, as far as that goes. As frazzled as I might appear at the moment, I'm not looking for someone to take care of me. I'm perfectly capable of doing that for myself. What I desperately need is someone who will support my parenting efforts—and the exercises that Dylan's speech therapist prescribed for him, like the one you just so rudely interrupted."

It was Heather's turn to look nonplussed. It had never occurred to her that a three-year-old would be subjected to such treatment as part of a prearranged professional treatment. That in itself made her all the more aware of her shortcomings as Dylan's intended caregiver. If she ever hoped to obtain her teaching degree, she was going to have to stop jumping to conclusions and transferring her childhood trauma onto other people.

"I-I'm truly sorry," she stammered, wishing there were some way she could start all over again.

Tobias shoved the splayed fingers of one hand through a shock of dark hair that was anything but a quiet shade. Brown at the roots, the sun had frosted its ends with golden highlights. The fact that he was in need of a haircut didn't keep Heather from wanting to test its texture with her own fingers.

"Don't be. You just had more success with Dylan in the five minutes you've been here than I have since his mother left," Tobias admitted.

Bitterness laced his words and desperation creased his brow.

Heather wondered what had happened to Dylan's mother. Had she left simply because of the isolation of living on a ranch miles from the nearest neighbor? Or through some fault of her husband? Had she run away feeling as manipulated as a child reaching for a cookie that could only be earned by performing some trick?

Whatever the woman's reasons, Heather felt a surge of pity for any child forsaken by his mother. Having been sent away by her own parents under the guise of developing her artistic gift, she understood just how devastating it felt to be abandoned by those who professed to love you the most. And how desperately one would work to earn and to keep their approval.

Tobias's words drew Heather out of the past and into a present that was growing more and more complicated by the minute.

"In case the agency misrepresented this job, Miss Burroughs, Dylan is developmentally delayed."

The last two words seemed to stick in Tobias's throat. Although Heather was tempted to give him a reassuring pat to help him continue, she refrained from touching him again. As she saw it, the biggest drawback to this job was not working with a developmentally delayed child but rather living in such close quarters with a man who made her feel so keenly aware of her own sexuality. Falling for Josef had cost Heather her love of music. Falling for this man could well cost her what was left of her self-respect.

Tobias cleared his throat and continued. "You come highly recommended, and I was hoping that you and Dylan might find a common bond in your mutual talent."

He gestured to the grand piano against the far wall. Its black polish glistened beneath the natural sunlight spilling into the room. It evoked in Heather such a mixture of conflicting emotions that she had to reach for the back of a chair to steady herself. Part of her longed to run her fingers over those beautiful ivory keys. And part of her had already slammed the lid shut on that part of her life forever.

"Your resumé indicated that you are an accomplished musician. Dylan has some talent in that area. At the age of three with no formal training, he can already play melodies on the piano."

The buttons on the proud daddy's shirt swelled against a chest that was already broad enough to tempt a woman to run her hands across its width, and to see if she could lace her fingers together when her arms spanned its brawny circumference. Heather gave him a challenging look.

"I hope you aren't thinking of shipping him out to a specialized school like my parents did to me. While twice Dylan's age at the time, I wasn't nearly old enough to deal with the pressures of such a performance-driven institution."

Tobias's eyes widened in surprise. He shook his head emphatically. "I have no intention of shipping my boy off anywhere. His mother may have felt restrained by family life, but I most certainly don't. Whatever you think of my parenting methods, make no mistake about the fact that I love my son, and I'll do whatever it takes to help him find his voice again. Even bribing him with a cookie if that's what the speech therapist recommends."

Though Heather blushed at the implicit reprimand, she nevertheless wanted to make sure they were clear on what she perceived to be the differences in their respective teaching approaches.

"As long as you don't expect me to use those kind of techniques myself, I promise to do everything else in my power to support you. I'll be honest with you, Mr. Danforth. I'm not much of a behavior modification fan."

"Fair enough, Miss Burroughs," he said, matching her formality with a sardonic lift of an eyebrow. "All I'm really hoping for is that you can strike a common chord that will help bring my son out of his shell."

Recognizing that his words were deliberately chosen for their symbolic value, Heather selected hers with equal care. Well intended or not, she could never bring herself to force a child to perform as her parents had forced her, inadvertently turning the lovely gift God had given her into a curse.

"I would be more than happy to help Dylan with his musical gifts—as far as he wants to develop them."

Tobias looked relieved. Elated.

"Good, that's settled then. The rest of your job is secondary to attending to Dylan. While I expect you to cook and clean, I'm not particularly fussy about either of those duties, if that helps any to put your mind at ease."

Heather didn't think there was anything about working for a man as handsome as a movie star and as rich as Croesus that could possibly put her mind or her traitorous hormones at ease. Still, his words and accompanying smile did help reduce her stress level. Applying for a job was in itself a new experience for her. Groveling for the position was out of the question. However, since Heather was hardly in the position to be setting conditions for employment, she decided to withhold the fact that her cooking experience was almost as limited as her time spent actually working with children.

"It's way past time for introductions, but just so you know, I prefer being called Toby than either Mr. Danforth or Tobias," he said, offering her his hand.

Again the jolt of lightning at his touch struck Heather's heart. Tingling all over, she tried to focus on the fact that such an affluent man preferred the less formal moniker. She liked that almost as much as she liked the fact that hard work marked his hands with calluses. Josef's hands had been as smooth as a child's, and though they had played her like a concerto, she suffered terribly beneath their cruel ministrations.

"You've already met Dylan," Toby said, continuing introductions.

Hearing his name, the child abandoned his bag of cookies and stretched out his arms to Heather. She did not hesitate to take the sticky little urchin into her own arms. He smelled of chocolate and baby shampoo and unconditional love. Dylan wrapped his arms around her neck and squeezed hard. The kiss he placed upon her cheek left its mark upon her heart.

The smile that reached Toby's eyes held no hint of jealousy.

"It looks like love at first sight."

Heather flinched. Although she knew he was referring to her interaction with his son, her father had said the exact same thing when he had introduced her to Josef. That relationship ended disastrously, and she had no desire to let her personal history repeat itself. She reminded herself to guard her heart against getting too involved with either Dylan or his father. This job was nothing more than a way to make enough money to get her feet solidly under her so that she would never again be dependent upon any man. That included her father.

And her one and only past lover.

It was little wonder the two were so inexplicably intertwined in her memory. Indeed, when Josef turned his back on her, so had her parents. Having done everything but legally disinherit her, they were under the impression that withholding their financial support would work even better than withholding their approval had over the years. Heather's decision to abandon her musical career and pursue a teaching degree hinged on being able to make enough money in the coming year to put herself through school on her own. It was imperative that she separate her personal feelings from her better judgment.

For the first time in her life Heather was going to have to count every penny. Luckily, Toby Danforth was a generous man. Whether warning lights were going off in her head like some spectacular Fourth of July fireworks display was of little consequence in the greater scheme of things. Whatever her instincts were telling her, Heather simply could not afford to walk away from this job.

"When would you like me to start?" she asked with a determined smile fixed on her lips.

"As soon as you possibly can."

Toby gestured apologetically around him. Though messy, the room was not so dirty or cluttered as to be impassable.

"I don't know if the agency told you, but my

housekeeper retired two weeks ago due to serious
health issues. To be quite honest, I'm in a real bind.
A ranch doesn't run itself, and taking care of Dylan
myself for the past couple of weeks has put me so
far behind that I'm not sure I'll ever be able to catch
up.''

He looked so overwhelmed by his circumstances,
so remarkably vulnerable and strong all at the same
time, that Heather couldn't help but feel the stirrings
of empathy. Not to mention the fact that she could
no more turn her back on his cute little boy than she
could walk away from a stranger bleeding on the
street. She understood how difficult it must be for a
proud man like Toby to ask for her help. The woman
from the employment agency informed her in a conspiratorial whisper that the child refused to speak
since his mother had walked away from them both.
Heather wasn't sure if it was possible for three
wounded hearts to be healed under the same roof,
but she had little recourse but to trust in the infinite
possibilities of tomorrow.

''My bags are in the trunk of my car. If you'd be
so kind as to show me to my room, I'd like to get
settled in and start right away.''

The relief written upon Toby's face was so genuine that it made Heather grow prickly all over. She
hoped in his exuberance that he didn't attempt to
pick her up like he had Dylan and swing her around
in the air. She was already feeling far too light-

headed to think straight. Toby's next statement did nothing to lessen that feeling.

"If you don't have a couple of nice dresses packed, we can pick some up in town over the weekend. I'm planning on taking Dylan to a family reunion of sorts in the next couple of days, and I'd really like you to come along."

Heather shook her head as if to rid it of cobwebs. Not the typical slow-moving rancher who drove his pickup down the road at a leisurely pace, Toby Danforth moved fast. Goodness, it was hard to process everything happening at once. She had been fired, rehired and invited to a family gathering all in the course of fifteen minutes.

"That won't be necessary," she said, struggling to overcome her innate shyness around large groups of people she didn't know. "While somewhat limited, my wardrobe should be adequate for any occasion. I don't suppose it should be too hard to get myself and Dylan ready for a little family get-together."

As long as it's no farther than the next county... and it doesn't involve getting on a plane, she silently amended. Her fear of flying had been the bane of a childhood dependent upon traveling long distances to perform across the country. Whenever possible, Heather made alternate arrangements involving buses or trains.

The tension in Toby's face was replaced by a smile as wide as the boundaries of his ranch. It was the kind of smile that made Heather want to attribute the accompanying flutters in her stomach to nothing more than first-day-on-the-job jitters. Certainly not to a sharp sense of feminine awareness making her ache deep inside.

"I'm glad to hear it," Toby said. "I'd suggest you pack light clothes for the trip. My sister says the weather in Savannah is unseasonably warm for this time of year. Did I mention we'll be flying out this Monday?"

Heather's mouth fell open in surprise as Dylan clapped his hands in delight.

Two

There was something so regal in the way the new nanny carried herself, it made Toby feel as if he were working for her instead of the other way around. Of course, it went without saying that much in the way of a superior attitude was forgivable as long as she was kind to Dylan. Youth and inexperience, eyes as gray and unpredictable as gathering storm clouds, a luscious figure and even a pair of tempting lips drawn into a thin, disapproving line when she leaped to the conclusion that he was teasing Dylan with that blasted cookie were all imminently forgivable.

And lamentably unforgettable.

Dylan never took to strangers like he had to Heather. He had always been reticent—often even around his own mother. The fact that Heather happened to be the catalyst for Dylan to utter his very first words since Sheila left was more than enough reason for Toby to set aside any reservations he might have about her. Since dear old Mrs. Cremins recently suffered a heart attack, he was desperate to replace her with someone suitable—someone willing to live in what Sheila had dubbed one of the most desolate spots in the entire world. Based on his ex-wife's decision to abandon country life and her family altogether, Toby seriously doubted whether he could keep such a beautiful, young woman like Heather around for long. He hoped Dylan didn't get too attached to her before she, like his mother, found her wings and left them to pursue a more exciting life.

Personally, Toby loved the isolation and stark beauty of the Double D Ranch. It was, in fact, the culmination of a lifelong dream to break away from his politically connected and sometimes dysfunctional family to stake out a life for himself and his son. It was a dream based on the American ideal of pride in owning something built with one's own hands from the ground up. The Danforths had roots so deep in the soil of the Old South that Toby's decision to relocate to Wyoming had initially been perceived by some of his relatives as an affront to the glorious memory of the Confederacy itself. Indeed, Toby's choice to make something of himself in a way completely separate from his family's influence was the equivalent of the Emancipation Proclamation that set an entire nation free.

Nestled against the base of the magnificent Snowy Range, the Double D was Toby's idea of heaven on earth. It was his belief that a man could think clearly beneath clear, cloudless Wyoming skies that went on forever. Such country had a way of putting technology and politics in their proper place. They challenged a person to rely on his wits and the goodwill of neighbors who still put their stock in a hard day's work rather than a volatile marketplace run by crooks and thieves—who somehow managed to protect their mansions while their small, unsavvy stockholders were forced to declare bankruptcy.

It was hard to explain why Toby had felt so strangled by the gracious living of Southern gentry. It wasn't that he didn't love his family, but rather that he'd somehow felt like a changeling growing up in his own home. Ever since he'd fallen in love with his first cowboy movie as a little boy, Toby knew what kind of life he was cut out for. And it wasn't one that involved luxurious golf courses and hoity-toity social events requiring black ties invented to choke the life out of a man so some Southern belle could drag him around by the end of it wherever she had a mind to go.

As eager as Toby had been to leave Savannah four years ago, he nevertheless felt it important to keep his family ties strong—if only for Dylan's sake. Devoted to his own father, Toby would do anything that Harold Danforth asked of him—including returning home to show support for an uncle of whom he'd never been overly fond and enduring the kind of stuffy formal affair that he personally deplored. According to his father, Abraham Danforth was on the verge of making a political bid for the Senate. At Uncle Abe's behest, Toby's father had called his own children together for a Fourth of July extravaganza at Crofthaven, the family mansion overlooking Savannah's harbor. The mansion had been in the Danforth family for over a century, and though it held no special, warm memories for Toby or any of his cousins as far as he knew, it was the perfect spot for an impromptu family reunion. Not to mention a fabulous backdrop to launch the political campaign of a man, who in Toby's opinion was more devoted to promoting himself than raising his own family.

Toby felt no jealousy for the wealthier side of the family. When his wife died years earlier, Abraham Danforth had promptly rid himself of his children by sending them off to exclusive boarding schools. Busy making a name for himself, Abe farmed them out over school breaks as well. Consequently, Toby's cousins spent many of their holidays and summers at his own childhood home making happy memories, and eventually coming to regard Harold as a surrogate father in place of the one who had so little time for them.

Toby didn't mind sharing his father with the cousins who were like brothers and sisters to him. Kind and loving, Harold Danforth was the kind of man that little boys wanted to grow up to be like and little girls wanted to marry. It was just one of the reasons that Toby was so anxious to have his son get to know his grandfather better. He hoped exposing Dylan to his extended family would encourage the boy to express himself more openly.

Heaven knows, whenever the Danforths got together there was plenty of talking and laughing and debating everything from the latest in politics to varying points of view in recalling their youthful antics. Toby knew his family would do everything in their power to make Dylan feel at home and bring him out of his shell. Bringing Heather along would give the child an anchor—and unfortunately free Toby up for any number of his sister's ill-fated matchmaking attempts....

Despite his repeated protests that he had little interest in dating again, let alone getting remarried, there was no doubt in his mind that Imogene would have every available belle lined up for his perusal when he arrived in Savannah. As much as Toby appreciated the fact that she had his happiness in mind, he wished his family would accept his decision to raise his son as he saw fit—as a determined single father who didn't need the added pressure of belonging to one of the most influential families in Georgia.

As much as he hated to spring this trip on Heather so soon, Toby hoped the extravagant salary he was paying would help ease any misgivings she might have about accompanying him. Her dismayed reaction to his invitation made him wonder if she had an aversion to flying—or just to spending time with him. Using Sheila as a gauge, it would appear he had that effect upon women in general.

Heather Burroughs certainly wasn't the grandmotherly type with whom he had been hoping to replace Mrs. Cremins. Nor the mousy sort of shy musician that made her presence easy to overlook. A man could mentally forswear the opposite sex all he wanted, but unless his body cooperated, there was little chance he could convince himself, let alone someone as tenacious as his sister Genie.

Something jumped in his belly at the mere memory of Heather whirling into his living room like a tiny tornado. In a pair of tennis shoes and worn jeans, with her blond hair falling loosely about her shoulders, she'd looked more like a popular rock-and-roll diva intent on smashing a guitar over his head than the classical pianist he'd been led to believe was refined and aloof by nature. The fire he'd seen in those smoky-gray eyes left him wondering if the right man might be able to spark an even hotter blaze behind that wall of ice.

Toby didn't like the direction his thoughts were

taking. This sparsely populated region of the West was not known for its liberal attitude, and Toby didn't like the idea of compromising this pretty young woman by placing her in a situation that might cause loose tongues to wag. Living under the same roof with a single man in such a remote area couldn't be good for a lady's reputation. Nor for his own standing in a community he claimed by choice as his own.

Nor for a man's libido, for that matter.

Especially a man who was so lonesome at night that he preferred falling asleep rocking his son than facing the demons that tormented his own empty bedroom.

The immediate necessity of hiring somebody to replace Mrs. Cremins overshadowed Toby's apprehension. The possibility that Heather might get his son to speak again gave him a sense of hope that had been missing in his life since Sheila walked out. While it was probably just coincidental that Dylan chose to speak when Heather arrived, Toby couldn't overlook the possibility that she was in fact the catalyst for that momentous event. He was willing to cater to Heather's needs if she proved to be a miracle worker.

Only time and patience would tell.

"I'm pleased to make your acquaintance, Dylan."

Heather extended her hand to the little boy who was looking up at her with a skeptical expression on his face. His father had left them alone to take care of pressing ranch business. Clearly hesitant to leave Dylan with a stranger, Toby promised to be back in time for dinner, one Heather expected she would have to rustle up after getting herself settled. The sound of the front door closing behind him echoed through the house.

"You can call me Heather," she told the boy, "or anything else you'd like."

She took his dimpled hand into her own and gave it a grown-up shake. When the woman at the employment agency told her that Dylan was developmentally delayed, she had made it sound as if the child was mentally handicapped. After meeting Dylan herself, Heather was convinced that there was nothing at all wrong with his mind. Behind those bright-blue eyes, she could see the cogs of his brain spinning, sizing her up.

"What are you thinking?" she said, touching a finger to his forehead.

A clever little monkey, Dylan mimicked the gesture by tapping softly on Heather's brow.

"Me?" she said, supplying the words for him. "Oh, I'm thinking that since you and I are so very much alike, the two of us are going to get along famously."

Heather didn't let the serious expression on his face deter her from holding forth on the subject. Dylan's special needs had drawn her to this job, rather than deterred her from it. Having made the decision to put her musical training behind her and embark upon a new career in the field of education, she was eager to test herself in a real-life situation. That way, if her father and mother were right and she truly was making "the biggest mistake of her life," she wouldn't have wasted any time and money at the university. Heather certainly hoped no professor would ask her to subscribe to the kind of degrading motivational theory that Dylan's speech therapist sold his father. Heather believed that such techniques were as counterproductive as the blistering lectures her teachers gave their pupils for "their own good."

Threatening to drown her, memories of Heather's own difficult childhood came flooding back. A musically gifted youngster, her early years were filled with unbalanced adult expectations and a grueling practice schedule interspersed with high-stakes performances that inevitably left her feeling just short of ever being good enough. Valued more for the prestige and potential income she would someday generate for her own ambitious parents rather than as an individual with a will of her own, Heather was shuffled off to an exclusive music conservatory at the tender age of seven. Hundreds of miles away from home, she grew up under constant pressure with little consideration given to her emotional well-being. By the age of seventeen, she was a weary veteran of the recital circuit and talent shows....

"Again..." Mr. Marion demanded over a pair of

*owlish glasses that intensified his disapproving
scowl. "And don't bother sniffling like some urchin
who stumbled in here off the street. Your parents
are paying a hefty sum for me to discipline you. Let
me assure you, tears are wasted on me. You will
play that piece again until it is right. Until it is perfect…"*

Heather preferred beginning her training with a
challenging student who knew his own mind rather
than a compliant one who accepted the scripts other
people had written for him without so much as questioning their motives. Like she herself had done until
so very recently. She had firsthand knowledge of
just how much easier it was to beat the vitality out
of a pup than to put it back in once its spirit was
broken.

"Don't worry, Dylan. I won't try to make you
talk if you don't want to," she said with a gentle
smile, assuring him that it would be far easier learning the rudiments of housekeeping and cooking
without a little chatterbox demanding all her attention.

"For what it's worth, I'm not much of a talker
myself. That's one thing we have in common. You
know, I wasn't much older than you when I was
separated from my parents. Whenever I was lonely,
I used to let music do my talking for me."

At that, Dylan cocked his head showing the first
real sign of interest in what she had to say. He gestured toward the piano in the corner of the room.

"Would you like to play a song for me?" Heather asked.

He responded by bouncing a wooden block off the hardwood floor where he had halfheartedly stacked them. Heather bent down to pick it up and aimed it at the base of his crooked-looking chimney. Not even the tiniest hint of a smile toyed with Dylan's lips as the structure toppled and blocks scattered in all directions.

"So much for the Learning Tower of Pisa," she said, amusing herself with word play that was lost upon her charge.

Sighing, she rose to her feet and approached the grand piano with an air of confidence that belied her true feelings. Having come to associate music with her broken heart, it took an effort to lift the lid from the keys and drag a hand absently along the keyboard. Just as Dylan was drawn to that melodic sound in spite of himself, Heather couldn't help appreciating the quality of the instrument at her fingertips. She didn't know whether Tobias Danforth was a musician himself, but the man obviously placed a high value on providing his son with the best money could buy.

She played a couple of scales and was not at all surprised to discover the piano was perfectly in tune. With her back ramrod-straight and her hands poised over the ivory keys in the posture of a venerate pianist, she gave the impression that she was going to treat Dylan to some classic rendition intended to soothe the heart of the most savage beast.

"'Peter, Peter, pumpkin eater, had a wife and couldn't keep her.'"

The melody that she played on those polished keys was universally familiar. A voice more suited to compositions by the masters rose to meet the exposed log beams overhead.

"'Put her in a pumpkin shell and there he kept her very well.'"

Abandoning his blocks, Dylan hesitantly approached the piano and sidled next to Heather on the bench. There he proceeded to plunk out the final three notes of the silly little ditty.

Laughing, she noted, "It sounds very much like your blocks plinking on the floor, doesn't it?"

The twinkle in his answering blue eyes was the impetus for Heather's next selection.

"'Twinkle, twinkle, little star...'"

It had been so long since music held anything but pain for her that Heather was surprised to lose herself in the kind of happy nonsense songs that demanded nothing of a pupil but a willing spirit and an eager heart. She wondered if she might coax him into a duet with the all-time favorite "Chopsticks." Delighted to have made even such a tenuous connection with Dylan, she hoped his father wouldn't mind if their dinner consisted of grilled cheese sandwiches and tomato soup straight out of the can.

* * *

The sound of music stopped Toby short as he stepped through the front door. It had been so long since he had heard anything cheerful echoing off the walls of his home that he wondered if he had accidentally walked into the wrong house by mistake. As much as he missed the smell of Mrs. Cremin's fabulous homemade meals wafting through the house at the end of a long day's work, the joyous noise that greeted him was far sweeter and infinitely more filling.

He followed the sound to an impromptu recital in the living room.

With their backs to him, neither Heather nor Dylan was aware of his presence, providing him a perfect opportunity to observe the interaction between them unnoticed. Why someone with a voice as heavenly as Heather's would want to waste her life as a nanny was beyond him. Toby didn't give that question more than a minute of his time. If God wanted to send him an angel, who was he to question Divine Intervention?

While Dylan wasn't exactly talking up a storm, it was the most animated Toby could remember seeing him in a long time. In keeping with the pattern established earlier in the day Heather played the beginning notes of a simple melody, and his son completed it. Like the subtle fragrance that Heather dabbed on her pulse points, her very presence seemed to somehow change the molecular structure

of the air itself. The oppressive aura that had domi-
nated this house since well before Sheila took off felt
suddenly energized with the possibility of healing.

The fact that the house was a mess and dinner not
on the table, nor anywhere near the stove as far as
he could tell, didn't damper the optimism rising in
Toby's chest. An empty belly was nothing compared
to the chronic worry that divorce had permanently
damaged his little boy.

"Daddy's home," he announced in a voice made
deliberately gruff to keep it from cracking with emotion.

At the announcement, Dylan flew off the piano
bench and into his father's arms. Such wild enthu-
siasm was foreign to Heather who watched the reunion with something akin to amazement. The sight
of this big man tossing his child in the air and catch-
ing him in a great, big bear hug made her heart beat
against the barbed-wire barrier she had so painstakingly built around it. A similar greeting from her
own father at that age would have likely sent her
scurrying to her room in fear.

Heather's reserve was partly due to her embar-
rassment about jumping to the conclusion that this
man could be a monster when it was obvious that
his little boy adored him. It was also partly due to
the fact that she had no desire to get any closer
emotionally to her new boss than was necessary to
maintain her present employment. Having just been
dumped by someone she trusted first and foremost

as a mentor and only subsequently as a lover, Heather was not about to risk her heart romantically again.

Just because at first glance Toby Danforth appeared to be Josef Sengele's exact opposite didn't mean there were no similarities between them. Past experience had taught Heather that men in general were not to be trusted. Strong-willed men like her father and Josef were adept at manipulating for their own purposes those they claimed to love. And Tobias Danforth struck her as one of the most determined creatures on the planet.

The only difference was that neither Josef nor her father showed the propensity for outward affection that Toby did. That was something to be counted in his favor. Assuming the silver-framed photograph displayed on top of the piano was of Dylan's mother, Heather was surprised that he hadn't done away with all evidence of his ex-wife. Undeniably beautiful, the woman in the silver frame spent the better part of the afternoon staring accusingly at Heather. As disconcerting as she had found that, Heather knew by the way that Dylan's gaze fell so often upon that lovely countenance that it was a comfort to him.

"I promise that I'll get around to the housekeeping tomorrow," she told her employer.

The apology in her voice was unnecessary.

"That's all right," Toby told her.

His smile was genuine and reassuring. That

Heather suddenly felt jealous of the toddler nestled so safely in those strong arms of his father came as a shock to her. Having given up romantic complications in her life, she could do little but let her emotions wash over her without outwardly acknowledging them.

"What you're doing with Dylan is far more important. What do you say I stick some frozen dinners in the microwave, and we can all relax in front of the television for the evening?"

Heather didn't know what to say. The invitation sounded tempting.

And dangerous.

The truth was she was ravenous. And for a lot more than the man was offering. There was no real explanation for why she felt like taking off running in the opposite direction other than the fact that something about this man put her into fight-or-flight mode. She didn't like what it said about her character that her body was inclined in the direction of the latter. Or that given the circumstances of her employment, avoiding Toby was going to be as impossible as controlling the chemical reaction that he set off in her every time he was around.

Heather's stomach answered for her, rumbling deep and loud in a manner that belied her dainty stature.

"That would be lovely," she said in a tone that gave away nothing of the conflicting emotions that left her feeling raw inside.

Three

―――

"**F**ake it until you make it," Heather repeated to herself again and again as she stared out the tiny window of the airplane that was waiting for permission from radio control to take her straight into the heart of the South and Toby's family.

That same mantra helped her through innumerable recitals and contests over the years. Clutching a small purse in her lap with both hands, she did her best to pretend she wasn't frightened out of her mind. Considering what an admirable job she had been doing of hiding that very fact from her employer for the past few days, it should have been a piece of cake. That the plane in which she sat barely qualified as a puddle-jumper didn't do much to calm her nerves. When Toby told her that his uncle was sending his private jet to transport them to the family reunion, Heather had envisioned something far grander than the single-engine Cessna idling beneath her more like a motorcycle than an actual means of transportation designed to leave the ground behind.

"Are you all right?" Toby asked.

He reached across what only questionably passed as an aisle to peel one of her hands off her purse and take it into his own. He found her skin cold and clammy to the touch.

"Is there anything I can get you to calm your nerves?"

"I'm fine," Heather said grimly through gritted teeth.

Her stomach lurched as the propellers began spinning. She covered her mouth with her free hand. Used to dealing with preperformance jitters, Heather dreaded the thought of vomiting into a paper bag next to a man who was showing her such touching concern. At least before a concert, one always had the option of discreetly slipping away to the privacy of an isolated bathroom.

Toby's voice was as smooth as aged whiskey.

"Why in the world didn't you tell me you were afraid of flying?"

Why not indeed! For the same reason that she couldn't tell him she was afraid of the feelings that living with him had stirred in her. Standing on the edge of his close-knit family, she felt like a starving child with her nose pressed up against a candy store window without so much as a dime in her pocket. Unwilling to admit that, however, Heather forced an excuse through lips drawn in a thin line.

"I'll be fine. It's part of the job. I understood that when I accepted it."

Glancing over Toby's broad shoulder, she shot Dylan a brave smile. It was lost upon the child whose head was bent over the traveling musical keyboard his father brought along to entertain him. Even a three-year-old was more at ease with flying than Heather was. She felt like an idiot for letting Toby guess just how nervous she really was. Not that he had to do any more than look into her eyes to peer directly into her soul.

"I'll be right back," he told her.

Heather forced herself to let go of his hand as he rose to his feet. She was grateful that he hadn't tried placating her with some platitude about there being nothing to be afraid of. That was how her father tried dismissing her fear of the dark when she was little. As had Josef whenever she waited in the wings for her turn to perform before a house filled with critics.

And right before he took her virginity from her.

Lies.

She was doubly grateful when Toby returned a moment later as promised, not with some condescending statement about air travel being safer then driving her car, but rather with a stiff drink in one hand.

"I hope you like whiskey," he told her, passing her a tall tumbler. "You strike me more as the type who'd prefer an umbrella and a cherry bobbing in a fancy drink. But since I'm not much of a bartender, this is the best I could manage before the pilot announces it's time to fasten our seat belts."

Such instructions were unnecessary on her behalf. Heather had securely buckled her safety device across her lap the instant she sat down—and read every word of the informational materials provided in the back of the seat in front of her. Just in case an ocean happened to materialize between Wyoming and Georgia, she was prepared to use her seat cushion as a floatation device.

The ice cubes floating in her drink offered more immediate comfort. Heather took a tentative sip. As its dark amber color suggested, Toby made it plenty stiff.

"I hope your relatives don't mind if I'm not able to stand up once we get there," she murmured with a diminutive little cough.

His responding grin was enough to melt those ice cubes clinking against her glass. Heather wasn't sure whether the warmth spreading through her body was due to her hormones or the alcohol hitting her bloodstream.

"Don't worry," Toby told her. "As far as I know, my uncle isn't basing his campaign on any protemperance stance. Which is a good thing, considering his own past.''

Heather raised a slender eyebrow.

''My family isn't exactly without blemish,'' he warned.

''Whose is?''

She took another dainty sip of her drink to steady her nerves as they began the long roll down the runway. Not one to pry, Heather was nonetheless curious. Local gossip connected Toby to a glossy layout of some fabulous mansion touted in a magazine last summer. Much of what had been said regarding the article was mean-spirited and envious in nature. She supposed such a well-known family would have to expect to have every flaw magnified in the press. She wondered if that was part of the reason Toby deliberately put such distance between them.

Since her own family relished any media attention and rushed to put their daughter in the limelight every chance they could, it was a stance she could uniquely appreciate.

''What's your family like?'' Toby asked.

Not sure whether he asked the question out of courtesy or as a way to distract her from their impending takeoff, she responded tersely.

''Quiet.''

Squeezing her eyes shut as the engines growled and the airplane strained to lift off, she hoped Toby wasn't angry at her brusqueness. Her stomach leaped as they became airborne and hovered somewhere between her head and her heart. Tiny beads of sweat popped out above her lip.

"Take another swallow," Toby commanded, squeezing her hand. His voice was far more reassuring than the remedy he offered.

Unfortunately, his touch counteracted that effect. Warm and strong, it suggested an intimacy that was not at all appropriate between an employee and employer. Heather fought to remember that she was hired to look after Dylan, not to engage in foolish romantic fantasies that left one feeling used and forlorn in their aftermath.

No matter how much Heather wanted to let go of Toby's hand, she could no more have done so than she could slow her racing pulse. In so small an airplane, one felt every air pocket and bump right in the seat of the pants. Looking out the window only intensified the feeling of dizziness that swept over her. The landscape below, parched by drought, may well have been the surface of the moon for what little comfort its familiarity brought.

"Turn around," Toby told her.

"What?"

He touched her nape with his free hand. She flinched, and her already stiff shoulders bunched up around her ears as he began kneading the muscles on either side of her neck.

"Let me give you a massage. Trust me, it'll help you relax."

Although Heather started to protest, the sensation

of his masterful fingers stroking her skin was too heavenly to forgo, even for the sake of pride. Toby took his other hand from hers and began to massage her knotted muscles in earnest. Heather expelled a deep breath of air and felt every muscle in her body relax. Suddenly the sensation of floating high above the world didn't seem nearly so frightening. She arched against his touch and tried to keep from sliding out of her seat. Her eyelids fluttered shut.

"That *is* nice," she admitted.

The sound of giggling in the seat behind her so startled Heather that she almost spilled her drink into her lap. Dylan apparently did not share her aversion to air travel. His reaction to hitting an air pocket was to pretend he was on a roller coaster. Toby looked pleased. While his son had yet to speak again since that first day when Heather arrived, laughter was definitely a step in the right direction.

"I'm afraid the only quiet one you're likely to find in my family is Dylan," Toby told her. "And with your help, I think we might be well on the way to curing that."

Indeed he was right on that account. There was a small army waiting on the ground in Savannah to meet them. As delighted as Heather was to be back on earth in one piece, she found the rush of people surrounding them with hugs and squeals of welcome almost as oppressive as the humidity making the air heavy and redolent with expensive perfume. Her knees were wobbly beneath her, partly from the effect of the miraculous concoction Toby had mixed up for her on the plane—and partly from a sense that she was being suffocated.

Dylan threw his arms around one of her legs. Oblivious to that fact, Toby took her firmly by the elbow. Heather felt like a wishbone being pulled apart. Caught in a throng of some of the most beautiful people she had ever seen, she reached down and pulled Dylan up into her arms. He clutched her neck as if it were a life preserver.

"And this darling angel must be my nephew," cooed a Southern voice so balmy Heather thought it warranted a fan.

A stunning blonde stepped out from behind that voice to hold her arms out to Dylan. Her eyes immediately gave her away as Toby's sister. The exact same shape, they were as vivid green as his were blue—with equal shades of compassion glimmering in their depths. Heather held her breath when Dylan hesitated. Already protective of him, she didn't want anyone rushing him too soon.

When he leaned into his Aunt Imogene's arms, Heather heard Toby expel his breath at the exact same time that she did. The tightness in her shoulders returned with a vengeance. It wasn't that anyone went out of his or her way to make her feel unwelcome as much as the fact that there were so many Danforths to try to keep straight in her mind at once.

"I'd like you to meet my sister Imogene and my brother Jacob. His wife Larissa. My cousin Reid, his wife Tina."

Toby's sister gave him a scathing look and corrected him almost the instant her name rolled off his tongue. "The last time anyone in this family called me Imogene, it was followed by both my middle and last name. I believe it was a code signaling that I was in big trouble, more often than not because of something my ornery big brother instigated."

Toby's embrace may have encompassed both his son and his charming sister without putting any strain on those big arms of his, but his laugh pulled on Heather's heart. She imagined the sound of that robust laughter mingling with that of a host of other Danforths, raising the rafters of a fancy mansion profiled in magazines that touted the lifestyles of the rich and famous. Heather's first impression of this prestigious family was far less stuffy than what she had anticipated. And while that was a relief in some ways, it complicated her relationship as Dylan's nanny.

As far as she knew, servants weren't expected to like their superiors.

Although Toby's introduction accounted for all the adults present, a couple of children had tagged along to watch the planes land and take off as well as to welcome Toby home. He scooped each of them up in his arms, promising them a special present from his luggage as soon as he unpacked. After collecting their bags they proceeded to a waiting limousine where Heather took a deep, cleansing breath and embraced the sudden sound of silence.

"To Crofthaven," Toby told the driver.

No more directions were necessary than the name of the Danforth family estate where Toby promised "kith and kin galore." He either chose to ignore the look of panic that flitted across Heather's face at that pronouncement or simply missed it in the middle of fretting about Dylan.

"I was surprised he went to Genie so easily," he admitted.

"And that he wanted to stay with her at the airport," Heather added. A dear friend was flying in on a commercial flight arriving any minute, and Genie offered to bring Dylan back to Crofthaven in her personal car. "Your sister seems very nice."

"She is," Toby assured her with typical big brother pride. "Actually all my relatives are. The worst thing about living so far away is missing out on family functions—and," he added with a wry grin, "maybe the best thing, too."

When Heather gave him an odd look, he hastened to explain. "Don't get me wrong. I love my family. It's just that I'm not much for black-tie functions like the big party Uncle Abe is throwing on the Fourth to launch his political campaign. I wouldn't have agreed to come home if Dad hadn't specifically asked me to. That man's sense of family obligation doesn't stop at the state line. Nor Uncle Abe's—

hence the private jet that flew us here—although I suspect his motives are less pure than my father's.''

Heather nodded her head in empathy. She had endured more than her share of the kind of black-tie events to which Toby referred, not to mention undue family influence about what she wanted to do with her own life.

''How were you able to strike out on your own without severing the family ties completely?'' she asked.

Having done everything in her power to avoid being alone with Toby in his home for the three short days that she had been working for him, this was the first time they had actually been together without Dylan present. Given the state of her hormones whenever Toby was near, it was far less awkward than Heather would have imagined. Like the TV dinner they had shared in front of the television that first night of her employment, it was amazingly cozy. If she wasn't careful, Heather knew she might start feeling like a real part of Toby's family. She was both flattered and flummoxed that her boss treated her more like a friend than an employee.

''My family accepts me for who and what I am. Luckily, they don't feel the need to mold me into something that I'm not. They just reel me in once in a while and remind me that I'm one of their own.''

''That must be nice,'' Heather said. Unable to come up with a better adjective, the wistful tone of her voice gave away the pain of her own family situation.

"It certainly makes me appreciate family all the more when I get the chance to come home. It's good for Dylan, too. A child needs to know that he's part of a tree with roots, not just some cottonseed blown across the continent."

Heather took the remark to heart. That was exactly how she felt. Like a seed tossed upon a hapless wind. She envied Toby the ability to do exactly what he wanted with his life without fear of being disowned for doing so. Dylan was a lucky little boy to be born into such a family.

She stared out the window. This was the first time she had ever been in Savannah. As the name itself suggested with its softly drawn syllables, it was a city of gracious living. The air was scented with magnolia blossoms as big as a man's open hand, dotting tree-lined streets that grew less and less modern the farther they traveled away from the airport.

The lush landscape of the South was a stark contrast to the wide-open spaces of Wyoming. They followed the Savannah River as it meandered through town. It reminded Heather of a grand old lady who was in no hurry to reach her destination but rather was intent on enjoying the journey itself. As the city gave way to the country, white-columned plantations evoked images of Scarlett O'Hara and a time lost to all but the blood of a civil war that soaked into the soil and permeated the very air itself. The voices of ghosts whispered through the Spanish moss hanging like tinsel from dignified oaks.

"What about your family?" Toby inquired, which pulled her gaze back into the vehicle and herself into the present moment.

Heather's voice was small.

"Not all parents are as understanding as yours."

Toby looked at her quizzically. "What do you mean?"

Naturally introverted, Heather wasn't inclined to speak of private issues, but for some reason she felt safe sharing a little bit of herself with a man whose eyes looked upon her so kindly. Perhaps a brief explanation might help him understand any perceived aloofness on her part when it came time for her to interact with the hordes of his siblings, cousins and aunts and uncles. She hoped he would approve a moment or two of the quiet contemplation that she needed to feel centered every day.

"As an only child, all the noise and confusion of a big family like yours is strange to me. Unlike your parents, mine pinned all their hopes on me fulfilling their dreams. I'm afraid I've disappointed them terribly."

"I can't imagine any parents not being proud of such a lovely, talented daughter," Toby said. "If they lost a child, they might well rethink their judgmental attitude."

His expression was so solemn, and his voice so

earnest, that it almost caused tears to spring to
Heather's eyes. She wondered who in his family had
lost a loved one tragically. All this talk of family
only served to rip the stitches from fresh wounds.
Just because this man had soothed her fear of flying
on the plane didn't mean he had shoulders broad
enough for more problems than his own. She tried
to make light of her pain.

"It's understandable given the amount of money
they spent on my training and…"

Heather's attention was momentarily diverted as
the driver pulled into a driveway leading to what
appeared to be a museum of sorts. A wrought-iron
gate with a curlicued *D* announcing the Danforth
estate swung open splitting the letter in two. She
gasped in astonishment.

"This is where you grew up?"

"Thankfully, no." Toby's voice rustled in his
throat. "The poor side of the family lives down the
road."

The lack of bitterness in his voice led Heather to
believe he was exaggerating his circumstances. The
grounds surrounding Crofthaven underscored her
initial impression of the prominent Danforths, por-
trayed in the media as a formidable and impenetra-
ble dynasty. The estate itself was so huge and the
gardens so elaborate that Heather surmised it would
take an entire army of gardeners working full-time
to tend the place. She wondered if the grounds ran
all the way to the ocean, and made a mental note to

walk the perimeter of the estate the first chance she got.

The main house, a large Georgian-style mansion, was listed as a historical landmark. Having been built over a hundred years ago, it showed no signs of neglect. Though it obviously had been modernized to include up-to-date electrical wiring and plumbing, great care had been taken to retain the original integrity of the property. Hollywood would be hard-pressed to find a better setting for an epic nineteenth-century saga.

"It's an amazing place," she said.

"It is," Toby agreed. "But not everything is as it appears on the surface. My cousins have far fonder memories of the time they spent at my parents' home than of their lives here. After their mother died, their childhood was marked by loneliness and some emotional neglect on the part of their father. Bricks and mortar don't make a home any more than money can necessarily buy character."

Heather couldn't argue that point. Out of the corner of her eye, she caught a slight movement that sent goose bumps crawling over her flesh. Beneath a massive oak tree, she saw the figure of a woman clad in ancient garb. She was too far away to make out much more than the dark color of her hair and her turn-of-the-century clothing, but there was no mistaking that the sorrowful-looking creature was wagging a finger directly at her!

In the blink of an eye, the apparition was gone.

Heather's fingers found Toby's arm.

"What's wrong?" he asked, covering her hand with his own.

She was grateful for the warmth of human flesh. Her own skin had gone deadly cold. Heather was on the verge of asking Toby if he, too, had seen the mysterious woman under the tree, but decided against it. She doubted he wanted to introduce her to the rest of his family as a loony.

Perhaps the woman was, in fact, part of a Civil War reenactment.

Perhaps a documentary was being filmed on site.

Perhaps Heather was overly tired from a long, arduous flight, and her mind was simply overcome by the aura of this incredible setting.

Or perhaps she was being warned from the grave to escape while there was still time....

Four

When the limousine came to a complete stop at Crofthaven's front door, their driver jumped out to open their doors. He was too late for Toby who was accustomed to opening his own doors and making his own way in the world without anyone's assistance.

"Thanks, anyway," he said, stuffing a generous tip into the man's hand. "And have a nice day."

As Heather stepped from the limousine, she tried to dismiss the eerie sense that some ghostly being was watching her. Surely it was only her imagination that chilled her skin and caused her to look over her shoulder. Letting the sounds of summer crickets and birds wash over her, she rubbed away her goose bumps and fixed a determined smile on her face. Dylan was eagerly waiting for them on the front steps along with half the population of Savannah, as far as Heather could tell.

They converged on Toby as if he were the proverbial prodigal son returning home. Contrary to her expectations, Heather wasn't shoved aside as much as swallowed up by the throng pushing them through the massive front doors. The Danforths were a jovial bunch who seemed more into bear hugs than the pretentious air kisses that her parents preferred on the rare occasions she was allowed to return home.

The apologetic glance that Toby cast in Heather's direction did not escape his sister Imogene's sharp green eyes.

Heather suspected little did.

At the moment, however, she was having trouble keeping up with all the names and faces crowded about. As if imploring a higher power, Heather cast her eyes to the high ceilings and ornamental fans so reminiscent of a Tennessee Williams production. Their gentle whirring stirred enough of a breeze to play a subtle tune on the chandelier sparkling overhead. As if sensing her discomfort, Toby put an arm around her shoulder.

She turned her face up to his as he bent down to whisper in her ear. ''Thank you for being here for

Dylan and me. You don't know how much it means.''

His breath against her neck was cooler than the air that greeted her when she stepped off the plane but it melted her on the spot nonetheless. Need revealed itself in the shiver that raced down her collar and out the ends of her fingertips. That same sudden need made her shift even closer to him to take shelter in the crook of the arm draped protectively around her. It made Heather want a great many things that were not at all possible given her status among the rich and famous gathered together in such an incredible setting.

Heather was so accustomed to Josef abandoning her at social gatherings, while he curried favor among the patrons and attended to his own adoring fans, that Toby's attention to her well-being caught her unawares. Why was he being so nice to her? she wondered. Supposing she must look terribly overwhelmed to warrant such attention, Heather resigned herself to making the best of the short introductions to come, if only for the sake of common courtesy. She was glad she wore dress slacks and a sleeveless seersucker top rather than the shorts she had been tempted to don in expectation of the South's famous heat and humidity. Breathing a sigh of relief that she was neither over nor underdressed for the occasion, she smiled at the man who had brought her here as a servant but who was doing his best to make her feel like a guest.

The crowd separated to let a slender woman step forward. Heather was reminded of Moses parting the Red Sea. Like so many Southern ladies, she was of an indeterminate age. Her blond hair was swept up in a tidy, timeless style, and she wore a simple chiffon dress of pale lemon. Except for the warm blue eyes that were Toby's, she looked just like Imogene.

"Mom!"

Heather studied the joy reflected in Toby's face as he swept his mother into his arms. The love between them was so genuine that a ripple of jealousy washed through her. She could not remember a single time that her mother ever greeted her in such an uninhibited fashion. Nor when she felt truly accepted by the woman who brought her into the world. In the Burroughs family, color distinguished blood from water more than any particular thickening agent.

Toby's father was only half a step behind his wife.

"Son!"

How a single syllable could carry such implicit approval was beyond Heather, but it most certainly did. Whereas Miranda Danforth was effusive in her greeting, Toby's father stopped just short of a hug, reaching out instead to take his son's hand into his. The handshake they exchanged conveyed something so sacred and honorable that it caused Heather to feel the need to turn away.

"I really appreciate your coming home on such

short notice at my request, especially when I know how busy you've been," Harold Danforth said. His eyes held a shimmer of deeply felt emotion.

Toby reached out to embrace his father for a moment that transcended time altogether.

"I wouldn't miss a family reunion for the world—whatever the reason for it might be."

Uncomfortable with such an open display of affection in light of her own family's threat to disown her, Heather wondered if she might possibly slip away and do a little exploring—of the house itself as well as of the raw emotions that were twisting her guts up into knots.

"And who might this pretty young thing be?" inquired Harold, directing his attention her way and banishing any chance of imminent escape.

Kind blue eyes regarded her from beneath a pair of bushy, heavy eyebrows.

"This is Dylan's nanny," Genie volunteered before anyone else had a chance to speak. "Her name is Heather Burroughs. You might remember her from a concert performance at the Civic Center a few years ago."

Surprised that Toby's socialite sister cared enough to remember her name, let alone reference any background information about her, Heather gave Harold a timid smile. Unlike her own father, who was of slight build and sharp temperament, Harold Danforth was at least 230 pounds and had a contagious grin. Shorter than either of his sons, he was nonetheless a big man. Both in heart and stature Heather imagined, if her instincts were correct.

"I'm pleased to meet you," she offered, feeling an immediate kinship with the man.

"The honor is all mine."

Words that might sound stilted on the page warmed Heather from the inside out. The man appeared to be a true Southern gentleman through and through. For the life of her, she couldn't imagine why Toby would want to leave the affection of such a loving family to strike out on his own. Fearing she might even get attached to these people herself if she wasn't careful, Heather was glad that her job would likely occupy her time for the duration of her stay.

It was impossible to tell which of the children running about were related to one another and which were merely friends of the family. With an estate of this size, it certainly wouldn't be any trouble accommodating a full-scale nursery school. Heather would cheerfully volunteer to run it, if it meant she wouldn't be asked to put in a polite appearance at Abraham Danforth's big campaign party. She'd had enough of strained social functions in which she felt compelled to vie for the attention of wealthy patrons of the arts. It would be nice to fade into the woodwork for a change.

Her thoughts were interrupted by the sound of a child's squeals as he came ricocheting toward her from out of nowhere. Gathering her wits about her,

Heather spied a boy of about Dylan's age sliding down a fantastic spiral staircase by way of a banister polished by the seats of children for over a century. Startled, she jumped aside, fearing if she didn't move that she might well prove to be the boy's landing pad. Taking the opposite tack, Toby stepped forward to catch the boy in midflight.

"And just who do you think you are?" he asked, peering into a face that took him back into time. The child was the spitting image of his brother Jacob at that age. "Peter Pan perhaps?"

The boy giggled. "Not Peter Pan—just Peter!"

His father stepped forward to ruffle the boy's hair. "Toby, let me introduce you to your nephew."

The pride in his voice was as unmistakable as his affection for the child. Unaware that Jacob himself had only recently discovered the son he didn't know he had, Heather simply assumed that Toby hadn't had the privilege of meeting his impish nephew. She liked the way he connected with all children, not just his own. She supposed such a man would have more than enough love to accommodate more than one child. Dylan would surely love having brothers and sisters to fill the void that his mother had left behind.

Not that Heather was eager to marry Toby off or anything. Just the thought of it brought a blush to her cheeks.

"The boys will be good for each other," she overheard Jacob telling his brother. "A few months ago, Peter was as reserved as Dylan and almost as quiet. Living together as a family has really brought him out of his shell.''

Older than Dylan by only a year, Peter grabbed the younger boy by the hand and urged him, ''Come on. Let's go play.''

When Dylan looked hesitantly at Heather, she smiled at the pair of them and offered to accompany them.

Toby placed a restraining hand gently on her elbow.

''If you'd like to stick around, I'm sure I can locate somebody to baby-sit while the adults get settled in. You look exhausted.''

''I don't mind.''

The thought of going with the children and escaping the familial chaos definitely appealed to Heather. Hoping to maintain a low profile for the duration of her stay at Crofthaven, she was eager to begin exploring the grounds herself. The possibility of meeting up with that mysterious lady beneath the big oak tree held a weird fascination for her.

Besides, Heather asked herself, what good could possibly come of a mere peasant mixing with America's royalty? She imagined such behavior could earn her the label of a gold-digger among Toby's relatives. Having been coached how to ''work a room'' by her instructors, Heather was hoping never to need to put that particular skill to use again. No matter how likable they might be, why should one bother trying to forge ties with people she was likely never to see again?

Heather could think of only one good reason: it would undoubtedly help her to understand Dylan better—and his perplexing father. For the life of her, she couldn't understand why he was looking so displeased with her at the moment. The stubborn set of his jaw didn't bode well for any argument Heather might set forth.

"It'll do the boy good to make some friends his own age," Toby insisted.

"Oh, let her go," Genie chided her brother before turning her attention to Heather. "Why don't you familiarize yourself with the place while we catch up on old times? I'm sure you'd be bored with the exaggerated tales my brothers are sure to spring on my new husband in hopes of embarrassing me."

Heather shot Toby's sister a grateful look. She hadn't expected anyone so privileged to make it easy for her.

"But," she continued in a honeyed drawl, "I do expect you to accompany Toby to the festivities. If he shows up alone, he's sure to start a stampede of unattached Southern belles in his direction that will upset Uncle Abe by taking attention away from the big political announcement he's scheduled to make."

Toby's protests fell on deaf ears as she continued teasing him. Their playful banter diverted

Heather's attention from the matchmaking glint in Genie's eyes.

She attempted a feeble rebuttal. "But don't you think Dylan will—"

Genie cut her off with the same mulish set of her jaw as her big brother's. The delicate-looking lady was living, breathing proof that Southern women hadn't acquired the *steel magnolias* nickname for nothing. Her husband Sheikh Raf ibn Shakir preferred working with his Arabian horses to socializing with the jet set, but he promised his wife he would make an appearance at the family reunion later in the day. He was looking forward to comparing training techniques with his brother-in-law.

"Don't worry about Dylan. He'll be just fine. Uncle Abe's hired a score of qualified baby-sitters for all the children in attendance. There will be everything from clowns to magicians to giant inflatable toys to keep them happily occupied during the festivities."

Like a cool breeze, Miranda swept into the conversation with a soothing presence that had settled so many squabbles over the years. "Of course you'll want to stay close enough by to check on Dylan if he needs you for anything, my dear. That would put my mind at ease, as well, but we would consider it a privilege to get to know you better. After all, as Dylan's nanny, we consider you part of the family now. And as such, we would be honored to have you stay at our home. It's just down the road a ways.

With all the political hullabaloo going on here at Crofthaven, it will provide a calmer atmosphere for us to get better acquainted with our grandson.''

There was no way of sidestepping such a gracious invitation. It made Heather feel all the more keenly her desire for a mother who went out of her way to make a stranger feel at home. Even though she knew that Miranda Danforth was simply being cordial, her words put a lump in her throat. All she had ever known of family was outrageous demands and strict compliance to what others deemed in her best interest. Miranda's suggestion that people might actually want to get to know her as her own person was flattering in itself. Her invitation to consider herself part of the family when Heather's own had turned so viciously against her was salve upon an open wound.

''If you're sure I won't be in the way,'' Heather said, lowering her voice so as not to betray her feelings on the matter. ''I would consider it a privilege to attend.''

A chorus of responses assured her that she would not be in the way at all. In fact, if the conspiratorial look exchanged between mother and daughter was any indication, Heather was about to find herself the center of attention whether she wanted to be or not.

Five

Toby refrained from tugging on the tie he was convinced was invented to maintain a choke hold on mankind in general. Though no longer the same little boy who so vigorously resisted being forced to attend such stuffy affairs as this particular fundraiser in the heart of old Savannah, Toby still preferred the smell of horseflesh to the cloying perfumes wafting through the lobby of the elegant Twin Oaks Hotel. Nor had his palate ever evolved enough to appreciate the taste of caviar, which was heaped in crystal bowls strategically placed around ice sculptures. He'd still take fried chicken packed in a picnic basket any day over black fish eggs that looked better suited for bait than dinner. Not to mention how much better a beer quenched a man's thirst compared to the dry champagne in the flute he held.

His glass froze halfway to his lips as an enchanting creature swept into the room. His heart thumped hard once, twice, three times in a rapid staccato before skidding to a complete halt. Had a pair of misty-gray eyes not sought his out at that very moment and shocked his poor heart back to working order, he might have made a complete fool of himself by spilling that fancy champagne all over himself and his brother Jacob, who was attempting to have a conversation with him.

"Then she said…"

Toby feigned an interested expression and nodded as if he was actually listening. He did not, however, take his eyes off the vision in blue who was making her way across the crowded room. Even though he'd mostly seen her wearing casual jeans and baggy T-shirts, he would have to be blind not to have noticed how pretty his son's new nanny was. The gown she chose for tonight's gala affair was not nearly so unassuming. Its satin fabric hugged her figure and accentuated her womanly beauty in such a striking fashion that every eye in the room was drawn toward it. Or rather to the woman wearing it.

In such a gown, Heather looked no more like a nanny than Cinderella looked like someone destined to sweep hearths for the rest of her days. If anything, Heather reminded Toby of an ice princess as she coolly made her way toward him. The way her gown so lovingly caressed her curves made him believe it had been designed expressly for her. Classic in design, the garment was a shimmer of sequins and beads that glittered with each step she took.

The hemline was deliberately angled from below one knee to midthigh on the opposite side. At five foot two inches tall, Toby had no idea Heather's legs could look so long and shapely in a pair of strappy silver shoes designed to make a man want to hang himself with his necktie. Her legs went on forever. He tore his gaze away from the sight only long enough to glare at the other men whose gazes were transfixed on the heavenly apparition floating across the wide expanse of the lobby.

Jacob jabbed his brother in the side and asked, "Where the hell's that one been all your life?"

"Presumably checking on Dylan," Toby answered dryly.

He took inordinate pride in the fact that he managed a swallow of champagne without choking on it. He drained the flute and set it on a passing waiter's tray. Not wanting his brother to see that his hands were shaking, Toby shoved them deep into his pockets and leaned against a marble column for support. He struck a pose of accidental insolence.

"That's not what I meant and you know it," Jacob countered. "Not all women are like Sheila, you know."

"Don't tell me Genie's twisting your arm to get

you involved in one of her harebrained matchmaking schemes.'' His groan conveyed more than words alone ever could.

Though the smile that crossed Jacob's face might be considered sly, his manner was so sympathetic that it invited Toby to open up as he used to when they'd shared their deepest secrets from their bunk beds after the lights were turned off.

"I don't believe in pushing a man into something he doesn't want, but I've got to tell you, little brother, that after fighting it tooth and nail for way too long, marriage is the best thing that's ever happened to me. I'm not much for giving advice, but I'm going to tell you something that I hope you take to heart. Don't let one bad experience scare you away from happiness. It's one thing to carve a niche out for yourself in the wilds of Wyoming and quite another to hide from life completely.''

Since those words came from his brother and because they were motivated by sincere concern, Toby chose not to hit him square in the mouth as he would any other man who would presume to chastise him. As it was, he simply stepped aside when his sister-in-law Larissa linked her arm through her husband's and drew him to the dance floor with an apology to Toby. The sight sent a tiny twinge of jealousy through him.

It was all well and good for Jacob—barely back from his honeymoon—to lecture him on the glory of wedded bliss, considering the fact that he had never been divorced. His marriage wasn't based on deceit. His wife hadn't lied about using birth control and deliberately gotten pregnant in hopes of "snagging" a good catch. Jacob had never had a hole punched through his heart. A hole so big that the wind whistled through it whenever he stepped outside. Never had a woman stolen his son's voice from him in her haste to move on with a more cosmopolitan life.

Or stolen his own faith in marriages like the one his parents shared for so many wonderful years. It was the kind of permanence he had taken for granted growing up. That his wife wasn't willing to work through their problems still stung. Toby didn't wish his brother ill. He just longed to find something as amazing as Jacob had. Fearing that was impossible, it was far easier to turn his back on love altogether than to risk being hurt again.

"Is anything wrong?" Heather asked, stepping beside him and studying the furrows lining Toby's brow.

She wore her hair loosely pinned at her nape and swept up in a style that was utterly feminine and flattering. A few loose tendrils framed a face that appeared unaware of its own beauty.

He shook his head as if to clear it of old cobwebs and resisted the urge to test the texture of a silken tendril between his fingers. "Nothing, except that you take my breath away. If you'll just be so kind as to stand beside me for the rest of the evening, your beauty should discourage all the single women my mother has lined up in hopes of fixing me up. Ever since the whirlwind romance that picked Genie up and deposited her in front of an altar with the man of her dreams, she's been wanting to duplicate the experience for me.''

Heather crooked an eyebrow at him. ''I take it you don't believe in whirlwind romances.''

Who would have thought that a man who looked so at ease in saddle-worn blue jeans could look so fabulous in a tailor-made suit? Had he the inclination, Heather supposed Tobias Danforth could make a living as a model. Not one of those pretty-boy types who bounced a beach ball over a volleyball net, he would be better suited to sales that required a man of rough edges. Heather could picture him in an advertisement that juxtaposed a close-up of the character lines in his face against the backdrop of the Grand Tetons. Or playing blackjack in Monte Carlo wearing the same tuxedo he donned for tonight's festivities.

Or in a pair of underwear that left little to the imagination and shamelessly played on his sex appeal to sell their product…

A glass of champagne looked like a tempting way to wash away the dryness that had settled into her throat like a desert. Heather nonetheless politely refused the one offered her. She met Josef in a similar setting and, as she recalled, complimentary champagne had done nothing then but cloud her judgment regarding the man who came to be her mentor first—and later her tormentor.

She could sympathize all too well with Toby's cynicism.

"You'll have to forgive me if I'm a little sour on the subject of romance at the moment," he told her.

"There's no need to apologize." Certainly not to me, she added to herself.

Having no desire to pry into her boss's private life, Heather hoped to be accorded the same respect in regard to her personal affairs.

Affairs being the operative word, she thought bitterly to herself, wondering why she hadn't simply worn a hair shirt for the evening instead of something soft and feminine.

Sensing the change in her demeanor, Toby obliged by changing the subject. "How's Dylan doing?" he asked.

Heather smiled when she thought of Dylan and Peter chasing each other through an inflatable playground that had been set up in an adjoining courtyard.

"You were right. He's still not talking, but he and Peter are inseparable, and they seem to understand each other well enough without words."

"Who's to say that relationships don't function best that way? Words damned sure didn't keep Dylan's mother from turning her back on the two of us, and I guarantee there were plenty of words between us."

Heather could tell Toby regretted his words as soon as he'd said them. His angry outburst explained much and softened her heart toward him even more. The fact that he kept a photograph of Dylan's mother on the piano back home made her wonder if he wasn't still in love with her.

"You didn't have an amicable divorce?" she asked softly.

"That's an oxymoron if I've ever heard one," Toby replied.

"Sheila's decision to leave tore our family apart. It was especially hard on Dylan."

"Except for the day you arrived, he hasn't spoken a word since his mother left."

"I'm sorry."

Heather's heart went out to him. Not demonstrative by nature, she didn't stop to think about the ramifications of putting a hand gently to the side of his cheek. Just shaven, his jawline felt smooth and solid against her palm. A gesture born of compassion turned suddenly reckless, producing shock waves so intense in the pit of Heather's being that they nearly doubled her over. Every nerve ending in her body surged in response to skin touching skin.

Toby flinched and drew a hand from his pocket to encircle her wrist. Heather braced herself. There was no doubt the man could have snapped her wrist in two, had he wanted to, or simply have exerted enough pressure to let her know she had stepped over an invisible line between employer and employee. He applied only enough to let her know he would not release her until he was good and ready to. Heather was not so much frightened as exhilarated in some unfathomably and undeniably sexual way. The strength in his grasp was matched by the sudden flash of desire that turned his eyes the color of thunderclouds rolling across an expanse of blue skies.

"Don't," he warned.

The band ended a slow song and paused a moment before playing their next selection. Beneath his hand, Heather's pulse was beating out a much wilder number. Shuddering, she nevertheless kept her eyes level with his.

A lively Cajun tune started up complete with twin fiddles, a zydeco and an accordion. Like the man who held her captive, it was exciting and dangerous on many levels. Her teachers and parents had done their best to keep her from such "coarse and sensual" music, but alone at night with her radio turned down low, Heather allowed herself to dream her own dreams while her foot tapped out the rhythm of such common, joyful tunes. As far from her classical background as the rambunctious Danforths were from her dispassionate family, such music stirred the imagination. And her blood.

Heather watched his gaze drop to her lips. She refrained from darting a tongue out to moisten them, licking them in an act of nervousness left over from junior high school days.

"Don't," he warned again. "Don't go playing with fire in the midst of dry timber."

Heather opened her mouth to protest but discovered that her voice had abandoned her. A more aggressive woman might have attempted wrenching her hand free—or maybe even landing a slap upon the features that looked at her with such arrogance. Struck mute, Heather could only watch helplessly as he drew her hand to his mouth and rubbed his lips across the center of her palm. To a curious bystander, it might appear to be a gentlemanly gesture. Heather knew better as she struggled to keep her knees from buckling. His mustache tickled her skin and ignited the very fire which he warned her about.

Nothing but a torrential downpour could extinguish it. Since the day she'd brushed crumbs away from that mustache, Heather had been intrigued by it. Having never kissed a man with a mustache, she couldn't help wondering just what it might feel like.

Up until now, Heather believed it was impossible for a person to forget how to breathe. Her involuntary shallow gasp was so evident of her bewilderment that it caused a smile of masculine awareness to spread beneath that intriguing mustache of his. It was almost as if Toby knew she was considering the effect of such kisses were they to be scattered at random all over her naked body.

Somewhere between the cold shivers and hot flashes that put her body into a state of utter confusion, a sultry Southern voice rang out.

"Why, Tobias Danforth, you rambling, contrary man. I was under the impression that you had fallen completely off the face of the planet."

Heather snatched her hand away and hid it behind her back like a child. A cloud of sweet perfume and taffeta stepped between them. A pretty thing, the woman had the distinct advantage of feeling completely at ease among the Danforth clan. She exuded the perkiness of a cheerleader. Heather bet she was the team captain.

Toby fell into the same antiquated pattern of speech used to address him. "Well, I declare. If it isn't Marcie Mae Webster, all grown up into a sophisticated femme fatale."

Marcie Mae's laughter tinkled like wind chimes. Heather envied her the ability to blush on cue. She imagined the woman would be just as at home in a hoop skirt as the designer original that she wore.

"I dare say I've changed a good deal since the days we used to go skinny-dipping down in the old sinkhole."

Unable to endure another sugar-cured syllable, Heather excused herself with the kind of euphemism a woman like Marcie Mae was sure to appreciate.

"I think I'll go powder my nose, if you don't mind."

Clearly Marcie Mae didn't mind at all. Her smile stretched her lips over a set of perfectly straight, white teeth. Taking Toby by the arm, she led him toward a group of old friends she claimed were just dying to see him again.

Heather tried not to smirk as Toby tossed her a helpless glance over his shoulder. That his apparent misery gave Heather a measure of satisfaction made her feel small.

The feeling was only intensified by stepping into a huge bathroom that reflected the sumptuousness of the rest of the hotel. Potted plants and cut flowers decorated sinks gleaming with gold-plated fixtures. The bathroom boasted high ceilings, a chandelier and several white wicker chairs positioned welcomingly around the room. Staring into one of the many gilded mirrors, Heather recognized the same panic-stricken expression she used to wear before becoming sick to her stomach before a performance.

Heather had never felt completely comfortable performing before a live audience. Few people could appreciate the cutthroat nature of her training. Even though it merely underscored the training she had received at home from her parents, such constant pressure had wounded her sensitive spirit so deeply that she had forsaken her musical gifts altogether.

Turning the cold-water spigot, she ducked down to splash her face.

Heather suddenly realized she wasn't alone in the bathroom. There were two women in a darkened corner of the room, and one of them was sobbing so brokenheartedly, it made her stomach cramp in empathy. Not inclined to meddle in other people's affairs, Heather intended to make a quick exit without getting involved. She would have made it, too, had not the other woman, obviously trying to comfort her companion, cast a desperate glance in her direction and mouthed a request for a tissue.

Heather took one from a hand-painted porcelain container and walked it over to them. The woman who took it looked to be about her same age. Wearing a beautiful white satin gown that accentuated a petite figure, she looked like a guardian angel. The woman shrugged her shoulders and gestured to the slightly open tall door.

"I stumbled upon the poor thing crying like this," the lady in white explained. She spoke with a slight European accent of some sort. "I didn't feel right leaving her alone in such a state. You wouldn't by any chance be an acquaintance of hers?"

Shaking her head, Heather edged toward the door. Just then the injured party raised her head from where it had been hidden behind her hands to reveal twin rivulets of mascara streaming down a face that was too young and pretty to be so angst-ridden. Not old enough to qualify as a woman or young enough to warrant still being called a girl, she was caught in that terrible in-between stage in which one fluctuates miserably between maturity and juvenile behavior. Heather guessed her to be the traditional age when Southern girls had coming-out parties.

The teen's voice quavered pathetically as she offered two convenient strangers an unnecessary explanation. "It might seem funny to you, but nothing I do is ever good enough to satisfy my father. Absolutely nothing."

"It doesn't sound funny at all," Heather assured her in a gentle, understanding tone. "In fact, I can relate to that all too well myself."

"As can I," added the lady in white.

Surprised to discover a common thread holding them together, the women studied each other. In addition to being approximately the same age, the two older women were of similar height and build. And behind their initial wariness was an inability to abandon someone in need.

Rather than watering down the girl's drawl, her tears had the exact opposite effect. Heather strained to understand the words that slipped out between sobs.

"Can you believe that my daddy actually expects me to throw myself at some old man in the other room in hopes of landing some big business contract? Have you ever heard of anything so vulgar?"

Heather wondered if by "old" she was referring to someone in his midtwenties.

"It absolutely makes me feel like a whore!"

The young lady's choice of words required yet another tissue to stem the flow of tears that started all over again. Feeling like she was caught in some Victorian time warp, Heather wondered what kind of father would deliberately use a child as a sexual pawn to advance his own ambitions. The answer came to her in a flashback of the day her own parents hustled her across a crowded room to introduce her to Josef Sengele, the master pianist famous for grooming young prodigies for stardom.

"I know how you feel."

It was not Heather's voice but that of the beautiful woman standing next to her. She made note of the flicker of pain that creased the perfect beauty of that face. Her voice held a sad ring of resignation. Eyes as brilliant as the emeralds on her ears softened as she put a hand upon the young lady's shoulder.

"Sometimes you just have to do what has to be done. No matter how unpalatable it might be, business is business and family is family. Come what may, you only have one father in this lifetime."

The teenager's sniffles stopped as she paused to consider the free advice.

"I thought I'd stay just long enough to appease Daddy without having to actually compromise myself."

Having attended innumerable stuffy functions on behalf of her parents, often as the featured attraction of the evening, Heather could certainly understand the desire to please someone whose respect could never be earned. She could not remain quiet on this point.

"Or…" Heather put a hand on the girl's other shoulder and finished her thought. "Rather than putting off the inevitable for years to come, years that wear away your sense of worth, you could take a stand right now and claim your life for yourself. Trust me. It's better to risk being disowned by your family than to disown yourself.''

Though her words were intended for the girl sitting between them, the woman in white turned as pale as her gown. She seemed genuinely moved. And oddly wounded by her words.

''You'll have to make up your own mind,'' the woman in white told the teenage girl. ''Whatever you decide, just don't torture yourself with doubts afterward.''

Heather nodded in agreement. Why she felt such a strong affinity to these two strangers was a mystery. She knew only that a delicate cord connected them for this brief moment.

When the bathroom door opened unexpectedly, admitting a pair of elegantly attired matrons, it jolted them all into remembering that they were not sharing confidences in the privacy of a home.

Sighing, the girl admitted, ''I'm tempted to just run away and avoid making any decision at all.''

Heather's life had been comprised of snapshots of so many fleeting encounters that she longed for a continued friendship, if only for this one strained evening.

''I really want to know how the evening works out for you,'' Heather told the distraught teen. ''Maybe we could decide on a time to meet and find a good spot to watch the fireworks later.''

The girl gave her head an apologetic shake, and

the lady in white choked on a dry, painful laugh as she reached first for her silver handbag and then for the doorknob.

"I doubt anyone will be able to miss them," she said cryptically before disappearing into the waiting throng outside.

Heather wished she had thought to ask for her name.

Six

Surrounded by a bevy of single women doused in warring fragrances, Toby studied his son's nanny from a distance. His worries that the shy little thing might not fit in at such an ostentatious gathering were proving completely needless. Heather looked so cool and sexy in that stunning dress that one might be inclined to think she was born to rule over these kinds of parties. The kinds of parties that his ex-wife had lived for. And ultimately left him for.

Toby washed away the bile that rose in his throat with a second glass of champagne. It lacked the bite of good, old-fashioned whiskey. But he doubted that even Johnnie Walker would make the sight of

Heather laughing at something one of his old class-
mates murmured in her ear go down any smoother.
Freddie Prowell was from old money, and though
his childhood acquaintance had always been a bit of
a prig, Toby had never felt any kind of hatred toward him before tonight. The sight of Freddie leading Heather onto the dance floor caused his shoulders to bunch beneath his suit jacket.

Where had she gotten that dress? Toby wondered.
It certainly didn't look like something one would
pick up off the rack for a special occasion. As Freddie's hand dropped to the small of her back, Toby's
fingers tightened on the stem of his champagne flute.
He imagined it would be as easy to snap the other
man's neck as the glassware in his hands.

Did Heather know that a backless gown could be
even more intriguing to the male population than a
plunging neckline. Toby's imagination kicked into
overdrive at the sight of all that creamy skin and the
realization that she wasn't wearing a bra. For all her
aloofness toward him over the past few days,
Heather didn't appear to mind a stranger groping her
in public. Not that it was any business of his. As a
free woman, she was welcome to dance the night
away with any number of drooling idiots lined up
to ask for the pleasure of her company.

For that matter, Heather could damn well return
to Wyoming wearing another man's engagement
ring if that was what she wanted to do—just so long

as she didn't leave him...er...he meant Dylan, high and dry without any advance notice.

Toby swore softly under his breath. He didn't bother waiting for the song to end before breaking free of the circle of women holding court around him. He simply left them to speculate on his rudeness and the certain direction his steps took him.

He tapped too firmly on Freddie's shoulder to be ignored. "Mind if I cut in?"

Considering that he managed to step between the two of them and wrap an arm around Heather's waist in one fluid motion, the question was purely rhetorical. As such, it required no answer but for Freddie to step aside. He did so reluctantly.

"My, but don't you look lovely tonight," Toby said, drawing Heather close and breathing her in. Her fragrance was a subtle mixture of daisies and the devil herself.

Batting her eyes at him, Heather donned an exaggerated drawl that mimicked Marcie Mae's. "I do declare, Mr. Danforth, such flattery could turn a girl's head completely around."

A smile played with the corners of Toby's mouth. Was it possible she was as bored with this party as he?

"Sarcasm doesn't become you," he remarked dryly, moving her toward the French doors lest anyone dare try cutting in on him like he had Freddie.

Heather turned the conversation to a safer subject

as the music switched to a slow, dreamy waltz. "The band is amazing."

Unable to take her eyes off the handsome man who held her, she wasn't quite sure when they left the ballroom floor and began dancing beneath a canopy of stars. It was less crowded in the courtyard and far quieter than inside. Beneath a night sky redolent with magnolia blossoms, a tender melody was carried on a breeze that did absolutely nothing to cool Heather off. She was on fire in Toby's arms. Overhead a meteor flashed across the sky reminding her of what happened to stars that burned too hot.

As tempting as it was to think they were alone, Heather knew that eyes would always be upon the likes of Tobias Danforth. Whether he cared for it or not, no matter how far he roamed from his childhood home, family ties cast him in the light of celebrity. His sister, Genie, had already warned her about the paparazzi. Heather had little desire to be featured in some scandalous rag bent on pumping up its subscription with innuendo and compromising photos. For all she knew, the full moon might as well have been a spotlight cast upon them.

Nevertheless, Heather turned her face up to Toby, and for a blissful moment allowed herself the luxury of floating away in the arms of a strong man. Toby defined his own life his own way, yet he was wise enough to preserve ties with a family that obviously loved him. She wished he would share his secret with her. Instead of asking outright how he managed such a complicated feat, she merely ventured an observation.

"You prefer marching to the beat of your own drum, don't you?"

Sensuous lips twitched beneath his mustache. "I know it's been a while, but I hate to think my dancing is so bad that I make you feel like you're in the infantry."

Heather shook her head. He was a marvelous dancer, moving with a grace that defied time spent in the saddle. Her body fit nicely against his like a pair of nestled spoons. There was no need to think about her own feet as he swung her to the periphery of the concrete pad and steered her onto the grass. She supposed his mother had forced him into dance lessons at an early age and imagined he had resisted mightily any attempts to mold a would-be cowboy into a proper gentleman.

"You know what I mean."

"One could say the same for you," he replied, searching her face in the moonlight for an explanation of how someone who moved so easily in high society would want a position as a nanny in the backwoods of Wyoming.

He had no doubt that a woman like Heather would soon grow tired of the simple ranch life that he so loved. His ex-wife claimed the isolation made her crazy. Once Sheila realized that she would never be able to cajole or badger him into resuming his rightful place in society, she couldn't renounce her wedding vows fast enough. One of the nasty rumors going around tonight's little soiree was that she was off in Rio with some European playboy and the two of them were spending Toby's generous alimony as if it were an endlessly renewable resource.

When the music stopped, he paused to consider a tendril of Heather's hair. Holding it between his thumb and fingertips, he studied each strand as if they were filaments of pure gold.

When the back of his hand brushed against Heather's cheek, the spark that had been teasing her imagination all night long burst into full flame. Although every instinct told her to pull away, to run away and not bother to look back, she remained rooted to her spot on the dewy grass. She fought to draw air into lungs that had forgotten how to breathe.

The fact that she and Toby were no longer moving did not lessen the feeling that the world was spinning out of control. A deft twist of Toby's wrist loosened the pin from her hair and sent it spilling around her shoulders in a shimmer of light that caught and held the moonlight. She might have protested against the injury done to her sophisticated hairstyle had it not been for a Roman candle exploding overhead, signaling the beginning of what was to prove a spectacular fireworks display.

"Look!" she exclaimed.

Toby didn't bother looking heavenward. His attention was fixed on the slender curve of an outstretched neck and shoulders so white they might have been carved from marble.

"I am looking," he told her.

Heather lowered her eyes to meet a smoky gaze, a smoldering source of heat that rivaled the rapid-fire explosions overhead. Having wondered what it would be like to be kissed by this man, she was overcome by panic when it became obvious Toby was about to put her imagination to rest.

This is crazy, she wanted to say. *You're my boss, and I'm your son's nanny. It isn't proper. And it most certainly isn't smart.*

Still, those warnings didn't keep her from leaning into him as he curled his hand around her neck and crushed her mouth beneath his. She would have fought against such unexpected roughness had it not made her so weak in the knees and left her desperately wanting more. His lips were firm, and she discovered that she very much liked the texture of his mustache against her tender skin. It did not tickle at all as she had read in foolish books she had hidden from her parents when she was a girl. But it did make her feel soft and feminine in contrast. And it left her wondering how that mustache would feel brushed against every inch of her body.

Resounding booms were coming more and more quickly as the fireworks display drew the crowd out of the lobby and into the courtyard. Appreciative ooohs and ahhhs filled Heather's head. Sparkles trailing across the sky were a poor imitation of the tingles racing up and down her spine. Great explosions of color mirrored the quick succession of emotions bursting inside her. She had been kissed before, but never had she tasted a man and been rendered insatiable by it. Wanting him to feel the same sense of powerlessness that she did, Heather held nothing back and responded wantonly.

The lady might look as cool as a Grecian statue, but trembling in his arms she was all heat and wondrously giving. Emotions that sparked off one another the very first time they met now caught on fire. Fanned by passion, they spread like wildfire as need raged through them both. Though supple in his arms, Toby discovered that Heather was not as fragile as she looked. Having tasted the forbidden fruit of his secret desire, Toby wanted nothing more than to tumble her into the shadows and make her his own. Such thoughts in such a civilized setting were utterly inappropriate. It was an obsession, Toby was sure, born of a prolonged period of self-imposed celibacy.

That didn't stop him from kissing her deeply and plundering the sweet depths of her mouth. Heather met the thrust of his tongue with her own inquisitive exploration. Toby's hands roamed freely over the warm, smooth skin of her exposed back. Moving his mouth to her neck, he thrilled to the beat of her pulse beneath his lips and the mewling sound caught deep in her throat.

"I want you," he confessed in a voice made raspy with need. "Right now."

There was no telling what Heather's response might have been had not a flashbulb gone off in her face. Her startled gasp was lost in the shouts of a crowd mesmerized by the effects of Abraham Danforth's elaborately planned fireworks display. Heather and Toby had been so engrossed in each other they hadn't noticed people were laying blankets down on the ground about them as others gathered on the veranda to sip mint juleps and admire the show.

Horrified to have a moment of weakness immortalized on film, Heather tore herself away from Toby with a sob. If it wasn't enough to be made a fool of by Josef and be forced to endure whispering behind her back in her home state, now she would be whispered about in Savannah, too. If she knew the paparazzi, her shame was certain to be on display in magazines by the morning. She could write the caption herself: Most Masochistic Woman in the World Falls in Love with the Wrong Man All Over Again.

Tabloids were sure to fly off the shelves at the little country store where Toby bought his groceries. By the time Dylan reached preschool, she supposed everyone would believe that his nanny was sleeping with his daddy. Angry at herself for succumbing to the charms of yet another man in control of her future, Heather turned and ran, less from the reporter who violated their privacy than from her mental admission that she was falling in love with Toby.

Blinded by tears, she didn't wait to witness Toby chase the unwelcome photographer down the sidewalk.

The Twin Oaks Hotel was virtually abandoned. Most, if not all, of the guests were watching the fireworks outside, and Abraham Danforth's political machine was gearing up to pass the proverbial hat around to solicit contributions to the cause. Heather had yet to meet the would-be senator, dubbed by the press as Honest Abe II. She doubted he would appreciate being upstaged in tomorrow's newspaper by a picture of her in a compromising position with his nephew.

She slipped around to a back entrance of the old hotel. The door stuck initially, but Heather had enough adrenaline surging through her blood to force it open. Making her way down a dimly lit hallway, she searched for some secluded spot where she could pull herself together and put that soul-shattering kiss behind her. If she failed to locate an unoccupied bathroom, she'd settle for simply finding the wing of the hotel that had been reserved for the children. Just thinking of Dylan's heartfelt hugs had a calming effect upon her.

One hallway led to another and before she knew it, Heather was completely lost. The place seemed to go on forever. With each step, the halls grew darker. Antique wall sconces that had been modernized with electrical wiring glowed with flickering lights intended to replicate candlelight. It was a touch too real for Heather, who was on the verge of turning around and retracing her steps when she caught a glimpse of someone at the far end of the corridor gesturing to her.

She looked remarkably like the mysterious lady whom Heather had spied under the big oak tree back at Crofthaven on the day of their arrival. As this was a formal affair, Heather could have easily mistaken a modern floor-length gown for the period clothing she thought she'd seen the woman wearing that day. In the shadowy light, it was easy to imagine quite a lot of things, including the draft of cold air that raised goose bumps up and down the length of her arms.

Nevertheless, Heather was drawn down that dark hallway.

"Wait!" she called out as the woman disappeared around yet another corner.

Hoping she was winding her way closer to the lobby, Heather gave chase. As she rounded the next corner, a scream died in her throat.

In front of her appeared a young woman with dark hair, very pale skin and eyes rimmed with pain. The shadowy figure seemed to float in the air. A golden locket at her throat glinted in the flickering light. Having never seen a ghost before, Heather nonetheless recognized this apparition for what it was.

Stumbling against the wall, she felt a drip of hot wax fall upon her shoulder from the wall sconce. She winced.

As tempted as she was to run screaming back down that hallway, both Heather's voice and feet failed her at once. Her heart pounded out of control as the specter stared through her with sorrowful black eyes. Without moving her lips, she relayed a message to Heather.

"Don't fail his little boy like I failed my charges...."

The voice resonating in Heather's head lacked the Southern tone which she expected.

"I don't understand," she whispered.

"Don't fail the boy," the woman repeated, blowing a frightening puff of breath directly in her face. "Or your own heart."

With that, she vanished altogether, leaving Heather to wonder if she hadn't imagined the whole ghastly encounter.

Seven

By the time Heather found her way back to the hotel lobby, she was questioning her own sanity. What other explanation could there be for a delusional encounter with the other side? Considering that she had been nursing a glass of ginger ale for most of the night, it certainly couldn't be attributed to alcohol. Heather supposed it went without saying that a hotel as steeped in history as Twin Oaks was bound to evoke eerie feelings in its guests, especially one overwrought by the prospect of falling in love with her employer.

That the same sad-faced woman would appear to Heather both at Crofthaven and Twin Oaks seemed further proof that her imagination was playing games with her. All that nonsense about not failing her charge and her heart was probably just her subconscious sorting through her conflicted emotions. Between overloaded hormones and better judgment.

The only other explanation was one that chilled Heather's blood and left her visibly shaking as she accepted her first glass of alcohol all evening from a bored-looking waiter. She tossed it back like a seasoned drunk and set the empty glass back on the fellow's tray in one fluid motion. Scanning the premises, she hoped the fireworks display was coming to an end, marking the official end of a long evening. She, for one, was ready to call it a night.

A deep masculine voice intruded on her thoughts. "Most everybody's still outside in case you were wondering."

Heather wheeled around and bumped into a solid wall of masculine chest. Craning her neck, she peered into the eyes of a tall, well-built stranger. That his brown eyes beheld her with amusement left her feeling both disadvantaged and tongue-tied. She hoped he wasn't expecting a response from her.

"It won't be long," he continued, "before Abraham Danforth makes his speech. After that, the party should begin to wind down, except for the diehards, who are certain to be here until the sun comes up."

Heather hoped nobody expected her to stick around that long. She was even willing to use Dylan as an excuse if it would get her out of here any sooner. Ever since they had arrived in Savannah, family members had been so eager to spend time with him, and he had been so preoccupied with his cousin Peter, that her services had scarcely been needed. Nonetheless, all Heather wanted to do right now was head back to Harold and Miranda's house and fall into bed. With any luck, the entire night would seem like a bad dream by morning.

Her voice was as shaky as the hands she hid behind her back. "Will you be among them?" she ventured to ask. "The diehards, that is?"

"Yes, ma'am," the man said in a strong, slow drawl. "I expect I will."

He didn't strike Heather as someone inclined to excessive partying. Yet he had just admitted that he would remain at the fund-raiser with the last of the diehards. She couldn't help but wonder why he was there. Alert as he was in scanning the premises without drawing attention to the fact, the man's emotions appeared as tightly coiled as her own. Feeling an odd sense of kinship with him, she offered him her hand along with her name.

"Michael Whittaker," he rejoined, growing suddenly solemn. "Good Lord, your hand is as cold as ice. Are you all right? You look like you've just seen a ghost."

"Funny you should put it that way…"

Heather's bones suddenly turned gelatinous. Michael reached out to grab her by the elbow. Concern illuminated his dark eyes as he led her to the nearest love seat and positioned himself next to her.

"What happened?"

Heather shook her head. "You'll think I'm crazy."

"I doubt that."

The hard look that accompanied those terse words provided Heather a strange sense of comfort. Still, she hesitated to relay the vision that congealed her blood and left her babbling to herself. Thinking back to that dark, haunted hallway, she took necessary precautions before baring her soul.

"You aren't by any chance a reporter, are you?"

The smile that broke across the man's distinctive features assured her that he found the very idea preposterous.

"A security specialist. Who better to trust?"

Indeed. What harm could there be in sharing a ghost story with a stranger at this late hour? What difference would it make even if he thought her mad? In a few short days, she would be a thousand miles away from here, well on her way to ridiculing herself for being frightened by a figment of her imagination.

Heather let her breath out slowly and took a chance on a stranger's seemingly benevolent curiosity.

"As a matter of fact, I think I did just see a ghost—if that's what you'd call it."

Seeing no sign of derision in Michael's manner, she continued haltingly.

"She was a young woman. Dark but not particularly menacing. And she was intent on delivering a message to me."

Michael leaned forward. "What message?"

Bolstered by the intensity of his interest, Heather described the strange clothing the woman was wearing and relayed her message word for word.

"I can't exactly say that I saw her speak those words, but I distinctly heard each one conveyed loudly and clearly in my mind. It's the second time I've seen her," she admitted. "First from a distance standing beneath a huge tree on the outskirts of Crofthaven, and right here at Twin Oaks not ten minutes ago."

"Miss Carlisle," he declared without hesitation.

It was Heather's turn to look startled.

"You know her?"

"Not exactly," Michael assured her with a crooked smile. "But the woman you described sounds exactly like the same mysterious lady who accosted me a few days ago asking me for directions to Crofthaven. I was several miles away from there at the time. After pointing her in the right direction, I thought I heard her mutter the single word *father* before she simply faded away."

Since Heather discerned neither malice nor ridicule in his words, she asked him to elaborate. The circumstances and settings of the appearances were sharply different, but the details regarding the specter herself were chillingly similar—right down to the gold locket worn on a chain about the ghost's long, white neck.

Giving her a reassuring hug, Michael apologized for having pressing business that he had to attend to.

"Are you sure you'll be all right?" he asked before he excused himself.

Heather gave him a wobbly smile. "I'll be just fine as soon as I get some fresh air to clear my head."

Toby was sorry Heather had run off before he'd been able to catch up with the reporter who made the mistake of interrupting the most romantic moment of his life. Undoubtedly she would have enjoyed seeing him grab the man by the strap around his neck and rip the film from his camera.

"Get lost, you disgusting little parasite," Toby told him before giving the fellow a kick in the pants for good measure as he slunk away into the shadows muttering about inquiring minds having "the right to know."

By the time Toby turned around to assure Heather that she need not worry about appearing in print any time soon, she was long gone, leaving him to search the crowd, all the while cursing the notoriety of the Danforth name.

He was unprepared for the surge of jealousy that exploded in his heart and flowed like molten lava through his veins at the sight of Heather enveloped in another man's arms. That Michael Whittaker looked nothing like wimpy Freddie Prowell did little to dampen the urge to ram a fist right through the other man's dark, handsome face. Toby had heard rumors that the man was ruthless, but he hadn't thought that reputation extended to the opposite sex. Years of hard physical labor outside a fancy gym would more than make up for the difference in their size. Toby might not be as big as his uncle's bodyguard, but he damn sure was a match for anybody when his testosterone kicked in.

He was just about to take his tuxedo jacket off and roll up his shirtsleeves when Michael Whittaker saved him the trouble by abruptly leaving. Heather wandered off in the opposite direction. Toby was familiar enough with Twin Oaks to know that a secluded terrace lay outside the very door through which she left. Perhaps it had been an innocent embrace explainable by any number of simple circumstances, he thought.

He curbed his impulse to make a scene. If Heather had been so distraught by the thought of their kiss gracing the pages of some sleazy tabloid, he imagined photographs of him involved in fisticuffs over her wouldn't set well with her, either. Nor with the rest of the Danforth clan for that matter.

Toby had no desire to ruin Uncle Abe's big night any more than he wanted to probe the intense feelings that his son's nanny evoked in him. Having openly professed to be done with women forever, he couldn't understand his own volatile reaction to seeing Heather with someone else, especially considering what a short time he had known her. Envy wasn't something that often came calling on Toby. His ex-wife bitterly claimed he didn't have a jealous bone in his body. Sheila's outrageous attempts to goad him into a green-eyed fit, intended to affirm her desirability more often than not, left her looking foolish in public and incensed in private.

Even now, news of Sheila's involvement with an international playboy only made him thankful that he and Dylan had escaped her exploits relatively unscathed. Unscathed, that is, if one didn't count his little boy losing his speech and his heart.

As desperately as Toby wanted to believe that it was merely gratitude he felt for Heather for helping his son, the kiss they shared beneath the fireworks shattered that illusion once and for all.

What had he done by initiating such a kiss?

Toby no more wanted a long-term relationship with a woman than he wanted to be tied to a life of leisure in Savannah. And yet the likelihood of being able to ignore his feelings for Heather once they returned to Wyoming was slim to none. Going back to a look-but-don't-touch relationship would tax all his powers of self-control. Hell, he'd nearly taken both Freddie and Michael's heads off this evening for just having the audacity to talk to Heather, dance with her and hold her momentarily in their arms. Considering that he prided himself on being level-headed and generally unruffled, it didn't bode well for his willpower.

He and Heather definitely needed to talk. The relative privacy of the terrace where she had retreated was as good as any place to initiate a conversation that was bound to be awkward at best—a conversation that could well pry the lid off Pandora's box. Toby wavered.

"There you are!"

Marcie Mae's voice rang out over the growing din in the room. Grabbing him by the arm, she tugged him in the opposite direction of the terrace demanding nothing less from him than his undivided attention.

"Thank you," Toby said.

"For what?" she wanted to know.

"For saving me from myself," was his enigmatic reply.

For the duration of their conversation, Toby kept an eye turned toward the dark doorway where Heather presumably sat in silence alone.

Taking up residence in a dimly lit corner, Heather did her best to work the ghost-induced chill from her bones. She wished she had thought to bring a shawl, but considering the time of year and the humid climate of the location, she hadn't dreamed one might be necessary. The ornate bench on which she sat was as cold to the touch as her encounter with the ghostly apparition. Heather had read that pockets of chilly air often announced that an unearthly creature was present, but never had she imagined the lingering effects of such an icy encounter upon her own human body. She longed to slip into a tub of steaming water and wash the whole experience down the drain before snuggling under the beautiful antique comforter on the bed that awaited her back at Harold and Miranda's home.

"I'm sorry. I didn't mean to be rude, but you bear a striking resemblance to someone I used to know."

The unexpected comment startled Heather from her reverie. Assuming the remark was directed at her, she looked to find the guest of honor himself, Abraham Danforth, had wandered upon her solitude. He was easily recognizable from the publicity posters scattered throughout the gala.

But he was not talking to her.

"Would her name happen to be Lan Nguyen?" asked a distinctly feminine voice.

The woman who stepped out of the shadows was diminutive in stature, no taller than five feet four inches in heels. Her dark hair glistened in the moonlight. Heather knew who Abraham was, but the woman was a complete stranger to her. Neither of them seemed to know Heather was there.

"Yes. Yes, it was," the older man responded. "How did you know?"

"Because I'm her daughter, Lea. *Your* daughter,

Mr. Danforth. The child you abandoned in Vietnam.''

Heather gasped silently. She hadn't intended to eavesdrop, and she wished there was some way to leave without interrupting. As it was, she hoped she wouldn't be called upon to administer the Heimlich maneuver upon poor Abraham. For once, the silver-tongued orator was at a loss for words.

Heather looked furtively around. She wondered if any reporters were within earshot. Or if one was perhaps setting Abraham Danforth up? Out of the corner of her eye, she caught a glimpse of Michael Whittaker slipping onto the terrace from a hidden door. She hoped she hadn't misplaced her trust in the man. When he motioned for her to remain quiet, she gladly deferred to his silent request.

Since Abraham hadn't bothered to dispute the claim, Heather wondered if the exotic beauty might not be speaking the truth. All this talk about fathers and their estranged children stirred up feelings in Heather that she was working hard to put behind her. Guests appeared to be conspiring with ghosts, breathing fire into Heather's ever present sense of guilt. As bitter as her relationship with her father had grown over the past couple of years, Heather couldn't imagine the courage it would take to walk up to a perfect stranger and introduce herself as his daughter. James Burroughs might have played the absentee patriarch for years and been a stern taskmaster, but Heather could nonetheless take comfort in knowing of whose flesh and blood she was conceived. She imagined life for abandoned Amerasian children must be incredibly difficult. How justifiably angry this young woman must be if she believed her accusations to be true.

Heather wondered how Abraham would ever explain to his grown children that they had a half sister. Or to the press, for that matter. Could his political aspirations survive such a shocking revelation?

When Abraham spoke again, his voice sounded like it was being dragged through broken glass. "Lan...survived? She survived the attack on her village? I thought she was dead. I—"

Lea didn't let him finish. "My mother is dead now."

Despite the defiant tone of her voice, she swayed on her feet. Michael Whittaker stepped out of seemingly nowhere to catch her when she fainted. Heather heard him mumble something softly in her ear before Abraham Danforth regained his composure and took control of the situation.

"Take her home, Michael," he said, sounding sincerely concerned. "Stay with her until I contact you. Until we can sort this out."

Heather couldn't imagine when that would be. Michael had mentioned that he was a security consultant. She hadn't guessed that he was actually Abraham Danforth's personal bodyguard. There was only one thing she knew for certain as the man of the hour visibly struggled to tamp down his emotions. By the time he was ready to return to the fund-raiser, he was composed again. The woman who introduced herself only as Lea was in good hands for the moment.

Before leaving, Heather gave Michael her tacit promise to keep what she had witnessed to herself, as he handed over the care of his client to the rest of his security team. She saw no reason to drop such a bombshell on Toby. He had plenty to deal with already and would likely be suspicious of such a disclosure as nothing more than unwarranted gossip. Abraham Danforth was a big boy, and Heather assumed he could handle his personal life without any interference from his nephew's hired help. It certainly wasn't her place to make such an announcement.

Besides, blabbing about the incident she had inadvertently witnessed would likely only prolong their stay in Savannah. As opulent as Savannah was, Heather longed for the solitude of the Double D—and the opportunity to explore her feelings for Toby far, far away from prying eyes, nosy reporters and well-meaning but intrusive relatives.

Eight

The scene Heather witnessed between Abraham Danforth and the woman claiming to be his illegitimate daughter strengthened her resolve to never let herself be used by a man again. Just as Josef had manipulated her for his own selfish purposes, Toby's uncle had apparently left at least one brokenhearted lover behind with nothing but an innocent baby to remind her of their time together. Heather was sure that the young woman's mother had suffered public and private humiliation while Abraham Danforth had gone merrily about the business of rebuilding his life and his empire.

Studying Dylan curled up in his daddy's lap as

their chauffeur drove them to the private local air-field where Abraham Danforth's personal jet awaited their return trip home, Heather realized that wasn't entirely fair. Some women didn't accept re-sponsibility any better than some men. It sounded as if Toby's ex-wife fit into that category. Not know-ing the details of their divorce, she thought it wise to refrain from making any judgments on the matter.

Still, looking at Dylan's sweet little face, she couldn't help but harden her heart toward a woman who for all intents and purposes abandoned her own child—and a family that despite their notoriety had been nothing but kind and accepting of Heather her-self. She hadn't heard anyone utter a solitary nega-tive comment about Dylan's mother. As much as Heather had wanted to categorize the Danforths as superior snobs, she genuinely liked Toby's family.

The day after the fund-raiser, Toby's brother Ja-cob, his parents, his sister Imogene and Dylan's young cousin Peter had said a heartfelt goodbye back at his parents' house.

"Why do ya hafta leave so soon?" Peter had de-manded.

Resting a reassuring hand upon the boy's soft hair, Heather waited to hear Toby's response as well.

"Even though I grew up here and I love my fam-ily very much, home for me is under the wide open Wyoming sky. Some people march to the beat of a different drum, Peter, and I just happen to be one of them. With any luck, you'll grow into the same kind of freethinker. And when the time comes, I hope your father will have enough integrity to let you go wherever your heart leads you—just like my parents did.''

Heather couldn't imagine what it would be like to have the kind of unconditional support that Toby took as his due. If she had been able to choose her own parents, she likely would have picked Harold and Miranda Danforth. True to her word, Toby's mother had never once made her feel a servant in their home. In fact, Heather felt more at ease in their presence than she ever had in her own home.

She swallowed against the obstruction in her throat.

Heather supposed all families had their problems. Looking at Harold and Miranda, one would never guess that tragedy marred what appeared to be their perfect life. In a private moment, Toby's sister, who insisted that Heather call her Genie like the rest of her friends, explained how their youngest sister Victoria had been kidnapped several years ago. Despite years of cold leads and discouraging statistical evidence to the contrary, the family never gave up hope that Victoria Danforth would someday return home. Given those heartbreaking circumstances, Heather didn't know how Toby's parents were able to let him out of their sight.

Thousands of miles out of sight.

A bump in the road and a flash of black alpaca

tore Heather from her present-day contemplations to the sight of a woman keening beneath the big oak tree. Heather's heartbeat slammed into a wall as their gazes collided. Time and distance dissolved as those black eyes bore into her. There was no mistaking the same specter that accosted her in the dark hallways of Twin Oaks. Nor could Heather ever forget the chilling edict she issued from the grave.

"You found your way back," she mused, recalling her conversation with Michael Whittaker.

"I like to think that I always will," Toby rejoined.

Heather didn't bother explaining that her comment hadn't been intended for him. She pointed out the window and, with an urgency that caught him off guard, said, "Tell me what you see over there."

He sighed before responding.

"My past."

The mysterious figure was gone.

With Dylan peacefully dozing, it seemed as good a time as any to ask Toby what he knew about the family ghost. He looked surprised when she broached the subject but did not disregard her inquiry out of hand.

"Stories have circulated for years about the spirit of a young woman hired as a governess to Hiram Danforth's children shortly after he built his mansion in the 1890s. All that's really known about her is that her name was Miss Carlisle and she was tragically killed on her way to Crofthaven when the carriage overturned in the dark just before she arrived.''

Toby paused to gauge Heather's reaction before continuing. He reached out to take both her hands in his and found them to be the temperature of ice.

''She's supposedly buried beneath that big oak tree over there.''

The blood drained from Heather's face. She didn't need to check any archives to know he was telling her the truth. It settled in her bones with a chill. She felt a connection between herself and the governess. Miss Carlisle had deliberately sought her out to offer advice as one caregiver to another. Whether one called herself a governess or a nanny made no difference.

''She spoke to me,'' Heather said in a small voice.

Toby offered her the warmth of his embrace, and she accepted it as eagerly as one shivering from the cold would wrap herself in a blanket. She was only vaguely aware of the fact that they had left the grounds of the Crofthaven estate.

''Do you think she might be trying to take possession of my body?''

Feeling her tremble, Toby gave her a comforting smile. His siblings and cousins used to scare the willies out of him with tales of the mysterious Miss Carlisle, and he didn't want to make light of the question. Nor did he want her to worry needlessly.

''From everything I've ever heard or read, she's

a benevolent spirit who never travels too far from Crofthaven.''

''Thank you for not thinking I'm crazy,'' Heather whispered in his ear before settling her head against his broad shoulder.

The rest of the trip to the airfield was uneventful. Savannah invited one to settle back and enjoy the verdant views. Heather couldn't help but contrast the lush vegetation to the drought conditions the West was experiencing. Here seeds needed only to be deposited by a gentle wind to take root and thrive in fertile soil. Back home, farmers had to work hard to scratch out a living from earth alternately baked, then frozen by elements that drove off all but the hardiest— and most persistent—individualists. Heather's father looked down his nose at those earning a living by the sweat of their brow, claiming that farming in the state of Wyoming was fundamentally a ceremonial occupation.

Toby reached across the seat to take Heather's hand into his own, sending an all-too-familiar frisson vibrating through her body. The goose bumps Miss Carlisle raised along her arms a moment ago disappeared as warmth washed over her in an equally disconcerting fashion. Heather took a moment to study the hand that enveloped hers. Strong yet gentle and marked by manual labor, Toby's hands did not look like those of a gentleman rancher whom her father might possibly approve. James Burroughs could probably forgive her daughter's

employer his rough hands and individualistic mind-
set in exchange for a taste of Danforth name rec-
ognition and social prominence.

As much as Heather wanted children someday,
she was grateful that Josef had not left her with a
baby to raise alone—like Abraham Danforth apparently had done to some poor woman half a world
away. Heather would have had little choice but to
remain dependent upon her parents' charity to make
ends meet. And such charity on their behalf would
undoubtedly come with shackles, rather than strings
attached.

She looked up into a pair of eyes as blue as the
sky that was to carry them home. Unspoken promise
glittered in the depth of those eyes. Her breath
caught in her throat. Was it possible that not all men
were like Josef or her father?

"We should talk," Toby said.

Heather wondered how he had read her mind. His
voice was a caress. It may as well have been her
heart and not her hand that Toby squeezed so reassuringly. The very tenderness of his demeanor was
her undoing. She hadn't slept the night of the fund-
raiser, wondering if he would ask her to resign her
position. Now, remembering how she had responded
so wantonly to his advances, she wondered if he
might propose a more carnal relationship that had
nothing to do with her job at all.

Heather reminded herself to proceed with caution.
Experience taught her that one's personal dignity is

a precious commodity. As such, it shouldn't be gambled away recklessly. The repercussions were often more insidious than one might first imagine.

She was curious to see how Toby's uncle Abraham was going to handle the scandal to which she was privy. As with the question of where her relationship with Toby was headed, she knew it was only a matter of time before things came to a head.

"Talk?" she repeated dully. "About what?" Her voice sounded scratchy. Raw.

"About us."

As much as Heather appreciated Toby's candor, she was surprisingly grateful to see the airfield come into view. It was an unusual way to cure her fear of flying.

"Couldn't it wait until we're on board and Dylan's asleep?"

"I suppose that would be wise," Toby conceded with a sigh.

Heather couldn't know that he was thinking back to all the discussions that Sheila postponed, always promising that things would get better without ever really hashing through the tough issues. She heard only the resignation in Toby's voice and assumed that the conversation he wanted to broach was not going to be pleasant. If it would make things easier on him, she could always quit.

Even if it meant giving up a job and a family she was coming to love.

Farewells in Heather's family were brief and dispassionate. The contrast between what she was used to and the tearful goodbyes Toby's relatives exchanged before they were allowed to board Abraham Danforth's private jet were startling. Ever vigilant about not intruding upon Toby and Dylan's private lives, Heather hastened to board in advance lest she be in anyone's way.

"Where do you think you're going?" Miranda asked.

The hurt in her voice stunned Heather.

"I thought I'd give you some space to yourself," she explained. Her own tone was conciliatory.

"I thought you understood that we consider you part of the family now." That said, Miranda took Heather by the elbow and guided her into the circle of Danforths.

Genie piped up with characteristic optimism. "I hope my brother has enough sense to make it official before your next visit to Savannah."

Presuming that "it" referred to a most unlikely wedding, Heather blushed so furiously that she would not have been surprised had her blond hair turned the color of strawberry wine. She did not miss the killing glance that Toby leveled at his sister. Shrugging it off with typical aplomb, Genie whispered something confidential in his ear.

"Don't hold your breath, little sister," Toby muttered.

The smile on Heather's face faded. Although she could only imagine what transpired between them, she assumed herself to be the butt of an unflattering remark. Miranda patted her on the arm.

"Don't mind them, dear. No matter how many times their mother has told them that it's impolite to whisper in front of others, they persist in misbehaving. You can imagine how I earned all this gray hair raising such headstrong children."

Heather could see little gray in Miranda Danforth's hair. She was truly a beautiful woman. Both inside and out. Indeed, her own mother made her feel more an outsider in her own home than Miranda had a guest—and a servant at that.

"I'm sorry," Genie said, looking truly apologetic. But then she took a deep breath and said in a rush, "I know it's way too early to start foisting anyone as ornery as Toby on someone as sweet as you, and he seems to think you have better taste than to ever hook up with someone as ill mannered as he is. But as someone just recently married to a man who not so long ago referred to marriage as the worm that hides the hook, I feel I'm in a unique position to point out what a mistake my thickheaded brother would be making if he let you get away."

"Genie!"

Howard Danforth seemed to be the only one able to control his daughter, with nothing more than a firm parental look. Though she ceased her teasing immediately, her eyes still twinkled mischievously. Heather wasn't sure how to react to earning the Danforth Family Seal of Approval.

Again Howard stepped forward to intervene. "We are very grateful to you," he said, looking at Heather directly and making her wish that her own father approved of her half as much as this veritable stranger. "What you are doing for Dylan—as well as for my son—is beyond price. We will be forever in your debt. Please come back and visit us again soon."

Surprised how much the invitation meant to her, Heather was at a loss for words. Then a little voice said, "Bye-bye."

The Danforths all gasped and looked at Dylan, who'd wrapped his arms around his father's neck.

"What did you say?" Toby said, stunned.

Dylan responded with a giggle.

"He said 'bye-bye,'" Peter repeated, shaking his head in disbelief that all the adults gathered about had simultaneously gone deaf.

Since Peter appeared to be the only one not taken aback by Dylan's words, Heather wondered if it was possible that the two boys had been conversing behind their backs for the past few days. Intermittent tears of joy and laughter surrounded the little imp's accomplishment. Though Toby claimed it was all Heather's doing, she was more inclined to think a combination of solid parenting and the unconditional support of an extended family was what prompted the child to speak up. That and an apparent eagerness to put his relatives' mushy goodbyes behind him.

"I told you he'd talk when he was ready. And without having to be bribed with cookies, either," Heather told Toby a tad too smugly a short while later as she cinched the seat belt around her.

She prepared for takeoff by staring straight ahead and doing her best not to hyperventilate. Dylan was still enthusiastically waving out the window to his family as their plane began to taxi down the runway.

"Give me your hand," Toby commanded, peeling Heather's fingers off the armrest.

His touch was at once both reassuring and unsettling. She found that she already missed Toby's family. That she liked them was really no surprise. They were as charming and gregarious a clan as anyone could ever hope to meet. What really surprised Heather was that they seemed to genuinely like her back. So naturally shy that she was often mistaken as being aloof, Heather was touched that Genie would actually broach the subject of marriage to her brother.

Given the baggage that both she and Toby carried from past relationships, the odds were not good that either one would be making a commitment any time soon.

Yet the calluses on the hand that held Heather's comforted her during takeoff. Her own hands, once unused to traveling over nothing rougher than ivory keys, would have to adapt to soapy water and pulling weeds in rocky flowerbeds and kneading homemade bread. Such working hands longed for the touch of a good man at the end of a day's work.

"It's going to be all right."

She knew Toby was referring to many things— Dylan's speech, the flight to Wyoming and the fact that his family's teary goodbye had affected him. Tears had been shed the last time Heather had spoken to her own parents, but they were the hot, angry tears of deep disappointment.

"If you renounce your music, you can renounce your name as well. And any monetary help from us, too," James Burroughs shouted. *"You will be as good as dead to me."*

Recalling how her father predicted she would either come crawling back, ready to live her life on his terms, or wind up as trailer trash with a half-dozen rug rats to support on a waitress's income, Heather wished there was some way she could adopt Toby's parents. The thought prompted her to ask, "Why would anyone leave such a family?"

"It's not like I'm disowning them," Toby protested. "I'm just following my own dream. They respect that and wish me well."

He sounded so defensive that it made Heather wonder if he practiced that particular speech for the benefit of other family members or to convince himself. She wished she could somehow convey how lucky he was to have such a supportive family.

"I'm glad," she told him. "Not all parents are as understanding as yours. It would break my heart to see either you or Dylan estranged from such good people.''

Toby gave her a long and searching look in response. He started to say something but seemed to think the better of it. Instead, he drew her attention to the fact that the plane had reached cruising altitude and suggested that she could relax now.

Heather was surprised that their conversation had so completely distracted her. Still, she was glad that Toby didn't let go of her hand as her fear abated. Looking out the window at the clouds, she pondered the fact that life in the South seemed to proceed at a more leisurely pace than what she was used to. The weather didn't necessitate that residents scurry from place to place in an attempt to escape the elements. That Toby deliberately chose to abandon the life of ease into which he'd been born mirrored Heather's own inclination to take a road less traveled. As beautiful as she found Georgia, the harsh climate of Wyoming suited her better. The weather there reflected her tendency to run alternately hot and cold on issues of the heart. Both extremes were potentially dangerous.

Only time would tell whether fire or ice would dominate.

Nine

Away from the glamour of Savannah and his family's resolve to marry him off, Toby Danforth was convinced he would be better able to resist Heather's allure. After all, few social events in Wyoming would require anything as glitzy as the dress she wore for his uncle's fund-raiser. Not that he would ever be able to get the vision of her in that slinky gown out of his head.

Or the memory of her lips upon his.

Toby was counting on the physical demands and grueling routine of ranch work to settle his libido so that he could do what was in the best interest of his son—and his pretty nanny. Namely, to leave her the hell alone. The last thing Heather needed interfering with Dylan's progress was him ogling her every time she turned around. The last thing Toby needed was for Heather to pack her bags in indignation and leave him in the lurch.

Deciding that his best course of action was to simply forget the impulsive kiss they shared beneath a shower of fireworks, he did not follow up on the conversation he'd initiated on the way to the airport. It was time for Toby to reestablish a professional working relationship with Heather and put aside any romantic notions once and for all.

The only trouble with that plan was that it might be easier to wipe the faces off Mount Rushmore than to erase the memory of their kiss. Despite his best efforts, Toby doubted whether things would ever be the same between them again.

Relieved that Toby hadn't decided to fire her, Heather did her best to cooperate with his unspoken plan. Back at the Double D, she went out of her way to avoid him as much as she could without being rude. First thing in the morning she fixed breakfast, which he wolfed down, and did not lay eyes on him again until the sun went down. Then he hurriedly ate the warmed-up leftovers from the dinner that she and Dylan had eaten at an earlier hour. Dylan hadn't spoken another word since his breakthrough at the airfield, but he made his feelings known by casting wounded glances in his daddy's direction whenever he stumbled in looking like he was single-handedly attempting to run a ten-thousand-acre ranch without the benefit of any of the hired hands on his payroll.

Secretly offended that Toby would go to such lengths to steer clear of her, Heather poured her energies into taking care of Dylan. Despite his continued reticence to speak, the boy was delightful to be around. His affinity for music matched Heather's own at his age and gave them a common bond on which to base a genuine friendship. Although his father's absence around the house left a void in Dylan's life that no nanny could fill, Heather used the time alone well. She worked with him on expressing himself the best way he knew how—through his music.

Watching his progress was gratifying. Reclusive by nature, Heather lost herself in the vast beauty of the Double D and in the sticky hands of a boy who she feared was coming to love her as a mother. She knew it was a slippery slope that she was treading but didn't know what to do about it. Heather could no more withhold her affection for the child than she could change the way her pulse skipped a beat whenever Toby was near. Just because they hadn't spoken about their feelings didn't make it any easier to deal with them.

In fact, it had the exact opposite effect.

Heather's determination to put her passion aside was becoming harder with each passing day. Having turned her back on her music and not having any close friends nearby, she didn't know how to deal with her complicated feelings. The joy Dylan derived from the melodies he produced on the keyboard took her back to a simpler time when she was able to express herself through her music. Unable to convey her own emotions, she did everything in her power to encourage Dylan to find his voice in his own way.

When she and Toby spoke, more often than not it was to argue over an adherence to the speech therapist's stringent behavior-modification plan to make Dylan talk. Heather had only met the woman once, but that was enough for her to know she didn't like her much. In her opinion, Miss Rillouso spent more of her time casting bedroom eyes in Toby's direction than in actually working with Dylan. As far as Heather could tell, the most the therapist had been able to coax from Dylan with her overly detailed plans was a grunt or two, and that was on the promise of some sugary treat to follow.

"If you earn at least twenty stickers on the chart I'm leaving with your baby-sitter, I'll bring you something special the next time I come back," Miss Rillouso promised Dylan.

Dylan couldn't have looked less bored with that proposition. Heather didn't take umbrage with the belittling term Miss Rillouso used to put her in her place. She merely tossed the chart in the garbage the minute she left the premises. Toby was furious to discover her treachery.

"If you're so sold on her stupid technique, you

do it,'' she challenged, handing him the sheet of stickers that went with the chart that Toby retrieved from the trash. ''I refuse to waste my time bribing Dylan when it goes against everything I believe about raising healthy, well-adjusted children.''

When Toby politely pointed out that he was paying her to do whatever he asked in regard to his son's treatment, Heather issued a dire warning of her own.

''If you're not careful, you'll create a monster out of that sweet little boy. A monster who won't take the trash out for anything less than a dollar or won't make good grades unless there's a reward attached to his report card.''

Toby bristled. He'd seen too many children completely hooked on external incentives to disregard her counsel out of hand.

''Helen Rillouso is a professional who came highly recommended,'' he protested. If nothing else, the outrageous amount he paid her to drop by the ranch every other week to work with Dylan attested to that reputation.

''I beg you to let him find his own voice in his own way,'' Heather countered.

Toby couldn't argue that her gentle approach seemed far more effective with his son than anything he'd tried in the past. Dylan seemed happier with each passing day. Still, Toby was a man who could afford to couch his bets. Even though Dylan was making progress under Heather's tutelage, he saw no reason to discontinue the program that Helen Rillouso had so painstakingly set up.

"All I'm asking for is a little support," he countered. "If you can't get behind the program yourself, at least promise me you won't deliberately sabotage the groundwork that's already been laid."

Heather thought long and hard before nodding her head.

"Out of respect for you, I'll do my best not to undermine your authority. I just want you to know that I think forcing the issue of Dylan's talking is as bad as forcing a relationship before someone is ready for it."

Toby gave her a searching look. He supposed that was her subtle way of telling him to back off. Short of sleeping outside with the grizzly bears, he didn't know how he could give her any more distance without compromising his relationship with Dylan. He sorely missed spending time with his son in his attempt to avoid Heather. In all the time he'd been married to Sheila, he'd never had such difficulty controlling his thoughts or his sex drive.

Maybe that was because she pursued him so shamelessly, lying about being on birth control so that she could get pregnant and force him into a marriage that he wasn't sure he wanted in the first place.

Heather was not like that. Though she had only vaguely alluded to it, her natural introversion had obviously been intensified by a negative experience with the opposite sex. If anything were to come of the attraction between them, Toby would have to be the one to initiate it. A man used to having women fall all over themselves to gain his attention, he found Heather a challenge he couldn't resist.

The fact that he was feeling more and more inclined to make the first move had little to do with his gratitude for the fine job she was doing. Instead, it had everything to do with the realization that against his better judgment, he was falling in love with her.

Heather would have to be blind not to notice the scorching looks Toby gave her whenever he thought she wasn't watching. Those looks alone made her blood run hot, her muscles clench and her pulse skitter out of control. Such confusing messages caused her to stumble all over herself whenever Toby entered a room. That the man was a perfect gentleman, always offering to help in any way he could, didn't make her job any easier. In fact, Heather had never worked so hard in her whole life—to pretend her boss wasn't getting under her skin during the day and into her subconscious at night.

Falling into bed at the end of the day, Heather was exhausted from rebuilding the crumbling wall that defined their relationship into employer and employee. No matter how high or sturdy she constructed that barrier during the day, by nightfall it lay in pieces at her feet.

Heaven knew she was no saint. After her disastrous fling with Josef, she had given up even considering herself a "good girl." It was no aversion to sex that kept her from following up on the powerful chemistry pulling her ever closer to Toby. It was fear, pure and simple.

She worried that going to bed with Toby would destroy their relationship altogether. Her experience with Josef had certainly proved that. Heather had little desire to be used and discarded again—especially since she so desperately needed this job. She needed the position not only to provide a sense of security but also a sense of self-worth. If she were totally honest with herself, she knew there was more to it than that. She had come to value her friendship with the man who had hired her to look after his son's physical and emotional well-being. Aside from the fact that the lingering memory of Toby's lips upon hers was a constant reminder to Heather that she was in fact a desirable woman, every day he was proving himself a funny, kind and surprisingly insightful friend. When she drew away, he did not push himself upon her like Josef had, either emotionally or physically. Instead Toby stepped back and gave her room to make up her own mind on any given matter without outside pressure. This all but ensured that she move closer to him on her own volition.

Tired as Heather was at the end of every day, sleep eluded her. When she finally did manage to drift off, more often than not her dreams were haunted by Miss Carlise. In the dreams, Heather was Miss Carlisle wearing a dress of black alpaca, and she would finger the golden locket around her throat. Inside was a picture of a man she did not recognize. Instinctively, she understood that this man occupied a special place in the governess's heart. A heart that demanded that truths be revealed in the lives of this man's descendants, generations cursed by the sins of a father.

That night, Heather's dream changed. Horse hooves beat an eerie cadence upon the black drum of night. It drowned out the sound of her own fists pounding upon the carriage door and her pleas for the driver to slow down. Somehow she knew that a dangerous curve lay ahead. A curve destined to end her life over and over again for eternity—unless the past could somehow be rectified by the present.

By an unsuspecting and perhaps even sacrificial soul.

A blur of images and the echo of her own screams woke Heather. She sat up, bathed in sweat. Disoriented, she looked about in confusion to discover herself safe and sound in a bed torn apart by her own thrashing. That a cry for help was still reverberating in her ears caused her to doubt her own sanity. It took her a moment to realize the sound was not in her head but rather emanating from Dylan's room. Fear grabbed her heart with stone-cold hands.

Springing from bed, Heather rushed to the boy's

bedside. The poor thing was in the grips of a nightmare that appeared to rival her own. Dylan woke with a start to see her silhouetted in his darkened doorway. He called out in terror.

"Mommy!"

Heather was at his side in an instant, holding him against her and soothing him with calming words.

"It's all right, Dylan. I'm here. I'm here."

Punctuated with sobs, a voice rusty from lack of use implored, "Don't leave me."

Those words ripped Heather's chest. Dylan wrapped his arms about her neck, clinging to her with a desperation that belied his tender years.

"I won't, honey. I promise I'm not going anywhere."

"Don't say that unless you really mean it."

The voice that issued that directive came not from the darling boy in her arms but from someplace behind Heather. Sitting on the edge of the bed, she swung her head around to see Toby standing in the very spot in the doorway that she had just vacated. Wearing nothing but a pair of simple white briefs, he was a vision of sculpted perfection. Heather had spent hours imagining his body's contours, but her imagination had been sorely lacking. Such a body deserved to be carved out of marble and immortalized for posterity.

Laden with genuine concern, Toby's voice was a caress in the night.

It was Heather's ruination.

Her own voice was surprisingly steady in response.

"I do mean it."

Ten

In a simple white nightgown, Heather looked like an angel at his son's bedside. Moonlight streaming through the window outlined the curves of Heather's body, revealing the shape and size of a perfect pair of breasts. The dark areolas of her nipples blushed deep pink beneath the thin cotton material. Toby grew hard with wanting her. He had never seen a sexier piece of lingerie than the modest nightclothes Heather wore. Nor a more desirable woman than the one whose eyes widened when she felt his eyes upon her. The enchanted melody she was singing, to help

Dylan find his way back to peaceful dreams, died on her lips.

"There, there," Toby crooned, stepping into the room to offer a frightened child the solace of his presence. "It's all right. Daddy's here. You just had another bad dream, that's all."

As this was Dylan's first nightmare since Heather moved in, Toby was greatly disturbed. Despite his best efforts to be all things to the boy, Dylan obviously still missed his mother. Dylan opened his eyes, reluctantly let go of Heather's neck and allowed his daddy to coax him back under his covers. Toby's hand grazed Heather's as he smoothed back a lock of hair plastered by fear to his son's forehead.

Together they comforted the child with gentle words and touches. The lullaby that Heather continued to hum soothed the child. Toby's nerves were pulled taut by parental worry—and a growing awareness of Heather's effect on his son. He couldn't help but feel jealous of the position that his son took nestled in her lap.

Under such tender ministrations, Dylan fell easily back to sleep. Heather tugged the sheet under his chin as Toby tiptoed over to the door. He held it open for her and, when she took her leave, closed it with soft finality before bending to scoop her up into his arms.

Heather put up no protest as Toby turned in the direction of his bedroom. Nothing had ever felt more right in her whole life.

Lacing her fingers around his neck, Heather held on tight. His flesh was warm to the touch. She buried her head into the crook of his shoulder.

The scent of Toby's shower gel mingled with the clean smell of linen from the bed he'd just left and the faint but heady aroma of his own body's musk. Intrigued, she kissed the strong column of his neck and licked the trace of salt left upon her lips. A feral growl rumbled from somewhere deep in his throat. The sound caused Heather to tremble as they crossed the threshold of his bedroom where he proceeded to lay her upon the very bed that she made for him every day. The covers were in a state of disarray from being thrown back in haste, but they were still warm from the heat of his body.

Heather spread her hair upon the same pillow that she secretly pressed against her heart before smoothing it out each morning. It smelled just as she remembered—like essence of man untamed.

Toby turned on a lamp situated in a far corner and flooded the room with soft light before coming to the foot of his bed where he gazed upon Heather with unabashed lust. She squirmed beneath his scrutiny and prayed he did not find her lacking.

"Do you have any idea how incredibly beautiful you are?"

Eyelashes, self-consciously lowered, fluttered open in surprise. Having learned early on that her talent was her greatest strength, Heather had seldom paid attention to her physical appearance beyond what was necessary in making a pleasing stage presence. Toby's voice was too raw with emotion and she believed that his words were not mere flattery. Nothing could disguise his hunger for her.

She watched in rapt fascination as he peeled off his briefs and dropped them upon the floor. Her breath caught in her throat as he proceeded to remove a small silver wrapper from the top drawer of his bureau and sheathe an erection that was well defined and beautiful in the dim light. Glad he had the wherewithal to think of protection when her own mind had turned to mush, Heather bit her lip. She hoped her relative inexperience did not disappoint him. Toby lowered himself over her, taking painstaking care not to crush her in the process. His tenderness caused tears to spring to her eyes.

"Why are you crying?"

Because I'm not sure I'm ready for this. Because I'm afraid I won't be able to please you. And that you'll think less of me for surrendering my body to you and that you'll toss me aside the instant you get what you want.

"I'm not," Heather lied. She removed the moisture from her eyes with a quick wipe of her sleeve.

Toby's eyes caressed her. "I'm not in the habit of forcing myself on women who are crying in my bed—regardless of whether they are naked or not."

How he managed the proper combination of sincere concern and gentle humor under such circumstances was a wonder to Heather. She smiled at the absurdity of his words through a blur of tears before leaning up to kiss him soundly.

The sweetness and passion of that kiss dissolved all apprehension as the world ceased to exist beyond the sensation of skin against skin. For all her shyness outside the bedroom, Heather was an uninhibited lover. She took delight in teasing Toby unmercifully. She ran the tip of her tongue along the fringe of his mustache, and when Toby opened his mouth hungrily to gobble her up, she proceeded to trace its outline with bold strokes.

His tongue sought hers in an unchoreographed ballet of give-and-take that left him breathing hard. Toby touched the blond hair spread out on his pillow like a golden fan as if to reassure himself that he was not dreaming. Propped over her with his weight upon his elbows, he stared down upon an angelic face incapable of holding back her feelings. Heather didn't have to speak words of love to him. He could read them in her expression.

Fully aware that Heather was not the kind of woman who fell into a man's bed unless she loved him, he did not want to break her heart. Wanting and loving were not altogether the same thing in his mind, and Toby knew that Heather deserved better than someone unable to commit to her completely. He didn't think he was emotionally prepared to make any promises beyond the fleeting pleasures and demands of the flesh.

Yet Toby could no more turn away from what

Heather was so freely offering than he could forgo breathing. Never had he wanted a woman so badly in his life. No matter how hard he worked his body each day, his every thought was consumed with having her. Sleep provided no respite from dreams that twisted him in clammy sheets, woke him abruptly and left him frustrated. Lust might very well damn him to hell forever and a day, but Toby did not have the strength to resist his own weakness.

Work-roughened fingers had no patience with the dainty, faux pearl buttons running the length of Heather's demure nightgown. Grabbing both sides of a scooped collar, he gave a little tug. Buttons scattered in all directions. Heather's gasp failed to cover the faint sound they made hitting the bedcovers, the floor and the nearby wall. Hoping he hadn't scared her, Toby made a feeble apology for his lack of restraint.

She responded with a kiss and guided his hands to the hole in the fabric that he'd made.

"Don't stop," she implored, offering him the comfort of a body straining to please.

Toby needed no more encouragement than that. Since the first day this woman stepped inside his house and pointed her stubborn chin in his direction, he wondered what it would be like to have her beneath him. Since kissing her beneath a shower of fireworks in a sultry Savannah sky, he couldn't stop dreaming of what it would be like to be inside her.

He struggled for breath as she tested his manhood,

gently squeezing it in her hands. Heather gasped again. Pushed to the limits of human willpower, Toby could wait no longer.

Despite his heartfelt intention to be gentle, Toby felt himself lose control.

Heather couldn't tell whether the indistinguish-able words upon his lips were an oath or a prayer as he plunged into her. She heard herself mimicking his language with soft, guttural sounds of her own— sounds that sprung from some dark, secret place inside her. There was no thought in their lovemaking, save a driving need to hold nothing back, as the passion that had been building inside both of them burst like a dam under unsustainable pressure. Raging, swollen waters swept them both away in a ter-rifying and oh-so-glorious ride.

Surrounding herself with him, Heather offered Toby not just her warm and willing flesh, but also feelings as real and enduring as the silver-rimmed mountains casting shadows through the open blinds. This acknowledgement came as a revelation. She dug her fingernails into the flesh of Toby's broad shoulders and discovered there was no way to keep from falling in love with the man who shuddered as he poured himself inside her with a moan that made her feel both small and powerful at the same time.

Heather squeezed her eyes shut and clung to the dream that he might someday love her back. That he continued to hold her and engage in tender af-terplay was a new and wonderful experience. Still, she knew better than to proclaim her feelings in bed. Such declarations tended to be brushed aside in the harsh light of day.

Josef had been the kind of man to tell a woman he loved her, even if he didn't, just to advance his own needs. Heather suspected Toby might have trouble saying those words even if they came from the bottom of his heart. Between the two, she far preferred the latter. Coaxing sweet words from a man meant nothing if he said them only in an attempt to pacify a petulant lover or soothe his own conscience. Wrapping her arms around shoulders slick with sweat, she reveled in the comfort of a body made hard by honest labor. Spent, he was hers alone until the morning light climbed the peaks of the nearby mountains, and brought not only a new day but also a new chance at rebuilding her life.

Eleven

———

Dawn light spilled across the mangled sheets of Toby's bed, bidding him to open his eyes slowly and count his blessings as he did every morning. The woman curled against his body in a kittenish ball was first among those blessings today. Staring at his sleeping beauty, Toby had to wonder if he wasn't still dreaming. His body's involuntary response to her silky skin against his convinced him otherwise.

That he could awaken in such a thoroughly aroused state after a night of the most intense and satiating lovemaking of his life was as wondrous as the realization that Heather wanted him as much he

wanted her. That she didn't seem inclined to demand
more than he was capable of giving at the present
added to the fact that she was already more than a
mother to his son, and made their relationship as
perfect as any he could imagine. He kissed her
awake with the aching tenderness he had been incapable of giving her last night.

"Next time I promise to go slow," he whispered
in her ear.

Stretching a body sore from a night of glorious
lovemaking, Heather smiled up at him in a way that
made his heart somersault inside his chest.

"I didn't find anything lacking in last night's performance, cowboy."

A sweet melody all on its own, her voice rivaled
the meadowlarks and robins that were noisily com-
peting for top billing outside. Never had a day
seemed riper with opportunity. Had Toby not a
ranch to run and a son to tend to, he would have
been more than tempted to spend it in bed, leisurely
showing Heather the many ways a truly dedicated
man such as himself could please her. As it was, all
that would have to wait until the sun set once again.

"We'd better get up and dressed before Dylan
wakes up and stumbles on the two of us in bed,"
Heather said, stretching languidly and wondering
when she would get around to explaining it to herself. "I don't think I'm up for that just yet."

"I suppose it could be traumatic," he murmured,

resisting the urge to tempt fate. "I'd hate to set his progress back any."

Though Heather nodded in understanding, her heart, which only a moment before was as light and spirited as a sparrow, fell like a stone to the ground. Reverting to her shy old self, she was out of bed in a trice. She grabbed her torn nightgown from the floor and pulled it around her, balling it in the fist of one hand. She may have been the one to initiate this particular topic of conversation, but it nonetheless hurt to think that her love could be considered disturbing at any level.

Was sex merely a prelude for all men to discard the women they conquered? The memory of Josef casting her aside for a new, improved and potentially more lucrative model came rushing back to haunt her. Determined to spill her tears in the privacy of her own room, Heather held her chin up high as she moved toward the door.

Toby reached out for her, pulling her onto his lap. "Not so fast," he said, pausing to nuzzle the back of her neck. "I said I intend to go slow with you, and I mean it. But that doesn't mean you need to rush out of here without giving me a kiss."

Heather worried that going slow only meant postponing the inevitable—a breakup that would cost her not only her job but also the last shreds of her dignity. God help her, she didn't think she could endure that.

Not when she was so completely in love with him.

There was no use in denying that fact any longer. Having already given Toby her heart, the only thing she knew for certain was that she would rather settle for a torrid affair with him than nothing at all. If it proved short-lived, as she suspected, she would cling to her memories to her dying day. The beautiful pictures in her head of their time together would always be her own to cherish and carry with her.

No one could take those from her.

In the time it took to turn around, Heather's jumbled thoughts sorted themselves out with the kind of clarity that eluded most people every step along life's predictable path. The kiss she gave Toby was sweet and full of promise.

It held no taste of the remorse clogging her throat.

There is a part of every woman that believes she can win a man's heart by completely satisfying his body. Heather was no exception to the rule. She opened her nightgown and let it fall to the floor in a puddle about her bare feet. Then she proceeded to push Toby back on the bed and straddle him. If they were to have only a short time together, she intended to leave a lasting impression upon him. One that would render him unfit for any other woman ever again.

Heather played him like a masterpiece. Lovingly. Her fingers ran over his most sensitive spots, evoking music from a place so deep inside, Toby was swept away with the profundity of it. His eyes widened to see this gentle, modest woman turn into a wild vixen.

His promise to go slow would have to wait to be fulfilled yet another time. Toby gave her all that she asked for and then some. His shaft was as demanding as the soft flesh that welcomed him home. He heard himself call out her name, filled his hands with breasts as soft as satin and suckled her until she came, again and again. Repeating his own name breathlessly over and over, Heather reveled in the glorious spasms rocking her body.

"I'm going to explode," Toby murmured through gritted teeth, as if regretting the fact that he could wait no longer to satisfy his own pleasure.

The crescendo carried him toward that explosion. Panting, he quivered in her arms, staring into a pair of eyes that mirrored his climax and accepted the warmth spilling into her with palpable satisfaction.

Holding her in his arms long afterward, the thrumming in his blood reminded Toby that he was a physical creature with needs, and that living life solely for one's children was always a mistake. Every man was entitled to seek happiness on his own terms. He believed that he, too, deserved to love and be loved for himself alone.

Love?

The word popped into his head, startling him. Could it be that Heather was looking for more than a physical relationship with him? Was it possible she wanted him without regard to what his name could do for her? That she might actually accept his dreams as her own? His arms tightened around her in the certain knowledge that one would have to be a fool to let such a woman go without a fight.

The days that followed were the happiest that Heather had ever known. Starting and ending her days in the arms of the man she loved was as close to heaven as she could imagine. In between, the time flew. She hummed while she worked and took enormous pleasure in the bouquets of wildflowers that Toby brought her every day. Dylan picked up on their happy mood and, though he still refused to speak, he smiled more readily, and the simple tunes he composed mirrored the joyfulness infusing a house that had only a month ago been filled with the sorrowful echoes of the past.

In helping Dylan express himself through his musical gifts, Heather was drawn back to the piano, as she had been when she was but a child herself. Now, however, rather than seeing the instrument as something that had once enslaved her, she began to rediscover her own love of music through the eyes and ears of a sensitive boy. Watching his little fingers move over the ivories, Heather came to understand that like love itself, when given of its own accord and accepted without strings, the talent they shared was truly a sacred gift.

Dylan smiled up at her instinctively. He nestled next to her on the piano bench and let the waves of that sweet melody wash over them and carry them both far away from troubles brewing in the distance.

Wiping his dirty hands on his work-worn jeans, Toby stood in the doorway of his house and admired the view in silent reverence. The curve of Heather's slender, white neck bent over the keyboard was enough to bring him to his knees. The softening light of the afternoon sun filtered into the room, casting a halo over her fair hair. The sight of his son snuggled up next to this miracle worker was something he wished he had the talent to capture on canvas for posterity.

Unfortunately, Toby was no artist. Nor did he share his son's musical gift. In fact, he once joked that he couldn't carry a tune in a 747 jet. His artistry and passion were reserved for the way he handled horses, a gift he had apparently been born with. He considered himself lucky to have parents who nurtured what others regarded as little more than a silly, boyish whim. That he was able to make a life around such a whim brought him great satisfaction—and the grudging respect of his neighbors. Toby had earned a name for himself among skeptical locals as well as breeders of national repute for the way he could gentle a horse without force. He didn't claim to be a horse whisperer. Still, anyone watching him could not help but be impressed with the way he com-

municated with even the most skittish of horses with
a calming touch and softly murmured words into the
animal's ear.

In all his years, never had he seen a more wary
creature than the one presently coaxing music from
his son's chubby little fingers. When the song ended,
a metronome on the mantel continued to keep time
to the blood throbbing in Toby's veins. He had faced
divorce with the kind of stoic discipline that char-
acterized his ideal of a strong man. Was it possible,
he wondered, that he didn't have to face the rest of
his life alone pretending to feel less deeply than he
did? Would the words *I love you* ever come as easily
to his lips as to his heart?

Where words failed both his son and himself, it
seemed music had the power to heal. He had read
somewhere that music could reach people with cog-
nitive disabilities. Even stroke victims who are unable to speak could sometimes sing the lyrics to familiar songs. Feeling emotionally disabled, Toby
worried he could very easily ruin everything by succumbing to the song of his own heart. Standing there
as a silent observer, surrounded by a feeling of utter
contentment unlike any he'd known before, he
longed to ask Heather to marry him.

He wondered if she would think marriage was
tantamount to tying a rock around her own dreams.
Heather had confided little about her past to him,
and Toby wasn't one to pry. Still, it didn't take a
rocket scientist to see that she had been badly

burned before and was leery of commitment in general. Toby had the feeling that she had one foot inside the threshold of his home and one firmly planted on a racing block outside. The last thing he wanted to do was scare her away.

Already devastated by his mother's abandonment, Dylan could ill afford losing the only other woman in his life he had come to trust and love. And Toby didn't think he could personally withstand losing the woman he had come to need as surely as a man needed air to breathe. He didn't know exactly when he had fallen in love with her, only that he had fallen hard. Just watching her now evoked such a fierce feeling of possessiveness that it would have scared a lesser man. He most certainly didn't want it to scare her.

Toby didn't know how Heather felt about taking on the responsibilities of instant motherhood. Or giving up her own dreams. Every time he thought about proposing marriage, he heard Sheila's mocking voice ringing in his ears.

What woman in her right mind would want to waste her life rotting away in the middle of such a godforsaken wasteland with a man who isn't smart enough to use his family influence to carve out a nice life for himself in the lap of luxury?

Sheila certainly had no compunctions about using her pregnancy to trap Toby into marriage. Nor walking away from that marriage once she discovered she would never be able to shape him into the gen-

tleman of leisure that she wanted him to be. There
was no doubt that marriage had left a bad taste in
Toby's mouth. He supposed it was only a matter of
time before Heather grew tired of the isolation that
Sheila claimed would make any woman stir-crazy.
And promiscuous if the rumors about his ex were
correct.

In Toby's mind, it was far better to try out a relationship without a binding ceremony than to risk
being so poorly used again.

So it was guilt, fear and bliss that competed for
top billing as both Toby and Heather sorted through
their feelings by day. At night the stars collapsed
about them as they sought ecstasy in the warm, willing flesh given to two souls desperately seeking a
permanent home in each other's arms. Come the following morning, they politely assured themselves
that they were only interested in the moment.

Secretly they both wanted much, much more.

''Would you mind taking Dylan into town for his
booster shot?'' Toby asked Heather over breakfast
one morning. ''I'd do it myself, but I just got a call
that Sun Dancer's arrival is going to be delayed. I
really need to be here to sign the paperwork when
he arrives.''

Sun Dancer was the prize stud upon which Toby
was betting a great deal of money to strengthen the
bloodlines of his stock. Heather knew the paperwork
was merely a front for the real reason he wanted to

remain behind. Whatever place she held in Toby's heart, she suspected his first love would always be horses.

"Far be it from me to deny one stud the pleasure of welcoming another to his new home," she quipped. "Besides, it'll be a nice change to get away from the ranch for the day."

Reminded of Sheila's aversion to ranch life, Toby flinched. "Under any other circumstances, you know that I'd volunteer to go with you."

Heather didn't pick up on the concern in his voice. She was happy to do him the favor and thought nothing more of it. How could she know that any mention of leaving the ranch for a change of pace sent shivers of dread racing through the man she loved? Or that he feared the same pattern of boredom and desertion repeated itself in such an innocuous statement?

Toby reached in his pocket and pulled out a wad of bills. He peeled off a couple of hundreds off the top and shoved them along with a credit card across the table at her.

"Why don't you buy yourself something nice while you're in town?" he suggested. "Maybe something pretty to wear. Or a piece of jewelry. And don't forget to stop for ice cream on the way home. Dylan hates shots, and it'd be a treat for him that might help offset his fear of needles."

Heather protested his generosity. "There's nothing I need—and nowhere really to shop for that matter.''

Toby's eyes narrowed as he repeated Sheila's thumbnail description of the nearest town. ''Just one cheap discount store and a couple of bars... I suppose it's not much of a place for a discriminating woman to make her mark on the world.''

Heather laughed. Marathon shopping had never been her idea of having fun. ''Good thing there's always the shopping channel on TV, then,'' she said, making light of his concerns.

An hour later, she was climbing into Toby's four-wheel-drive crew cab after securing Dylan in the child seat next to her. Toby put his hands around her waist and helped her up into the vehicle without having to strain himself any. Heather couldn't refrain from running her hands along the muscles of his arms and letting them rest there.

''You do look good in a cowboy hat,'' she said, ruffling the short hair curling at the base of his neck.

It amused her that he thought it too long if it reached the top of his collar. Because she thought he had a particularly kissable neck, she would never complain about its length. Toby returned the compliment by taking the hat off his head and placing it on hers. The hatband left a workingman's mark upon his hair that Heather smoothed out with loving care.

''You, too,'' he murmured and lowered his voice to add, ''but you look even better in nothing at all.''

They kissed. In the background a glorious backdrop of mountains shimmered in the rising heat, and any fears about the future dissipated like a dessert mirage. Heather had grown so used to his mustache that it no longer tickled—any part of her body. She cherished the warmth of his lips upon hers and wouldn't give up that feeling a second before she had to. Her entire world pivoted around this solid hunk of man. She clung to him as if fearing she might go spinning off into the cosmos if she ever let go.

In the distance a trailer kicked up a cloud of dust marking Sun Dancer's arrival. Toby's eyes lit up. Sighing, Heather glanced at her watch and put the vehicle in gear.

"I can't help feeling dwarfed by this monster truck," she admitted. "I should pack a stepladder so I can get in and out by myself."

"A sporty little car just doesn't have much place on a ranch," Toby apologized, leaning into the open window and trying to memorize the heavenly smell of the perfume she was wearing. "But if that's what you want, I'd buy one for you in a heartbeat."

Heather laughed and kissed him again before sneaking a peek at Dylan in the seat beside her. The boy didn't seem in the least traumatized by the affection between them. In fact, he wore a great big grin as he held out his arms and demanded a hug from his father, too. Heather made herself turn away from the poignant scene. It was dangerous to let herself feel like she was a part of a real family.

Bouncing down the gravel road a few minutes later, Heather reconsidered Toby's offer to buy her some new clothes. Perhaps that comment was just his way of letting her know he was tired of seeing her wearing the same few shirts and jeans that comprised the majority of her wardrobe. Feeling far from the glamorous picture of the ex-wife still gracing the top of the piano, she hoped Toby was not embarrassed by her simple attire.

Or by his relationship with her.

Ultimately it wasn't the size of the town that left Heather feeling small but rather the size of the minds that inhabited it. Dylan held up well under the practiced and blessedly quick shot that the doctor administered. Promising a brave boy a reward, she pulled into the dusty parking lot of the Whistle Stop Café a short while later and told Dylan that he could order whatever he liked once they were inside.

That the railroad had long ago bypassed the Whistle Stop didn't warrant a name change according to the string of owners who managed the landmark, through the subsequent booms and busts that pockmarked Wyoming's history. The latest proprietor boasted a bottomless cup of coffee and the best pie in the whole darn county. It also was the roosting spot for locals to catch up on gossip and bemoan the price of cattle on any given day. The noon rush consisted of a dozen or so customers.

As they took their seat at a well-worn booth, Heather had the oddest feeling that everyone in the place was looking at her. Brushing off the feeling as pure paranoia, she ordered coffee and an extra spoon for the brownie sundae Dylan ordered. Their waitress assured them it was twice as much as Dylan could dream of eating by himself. The woman, whose name tag announced her to the world as Nancy, was a big-boned blonde with nice features and a hairstyle popular in the previous decade.

"That her?" asked one of the fellows sitting on a revolving stool at the counter as Nancy refilled his coffee on her way to the refrigerator.

Despite the sizable wad of chew pinched between the man's lip and jaw, he spoke clearly and loud enough for Heather to hear.

"Shhh," the waitress told him returning with their order.

She discreetly closed the magazine that he had open on the counter. She then proceeded to put a huge scoop of vanilla ice cream on top of a saucer-size brownie, dripped hot fudge over it, gave it a noisy squirt of whipped cream from a can and topped off the caloric nightmare with a single maraschino cherry.

Nancy placed the gooey concoction before Dylan a moment later. His eyes grew wide in appreciation.

"Still not talking, huh?" the woman inquired. Concern creased her brow.

Heather allowed Dylan time enough to respond

should he have chosen to do so before supplying an answer for him. "I'm afraid not."

She assumed Nancy must know Dylan through a previous association with Toby and thought it nice of her to ask. A couple of bites of chocolate was enough to satisfy Heather's craving for something sweet. Setting down her spoon, she scanned a nearby rack of magazines and newspapers, hoping to find something to occupy her time while Dylan made a charming mess of himself. One publication in particular caught her eye—and by the looks of the prominently displayed, and nearly empty space, on that rack—everyone else's as well.

Exclusive Photos of Danforth Family Fourth of July Bash! was proudly proclaimed in bold print across its banner.

Heather snatched up the only remaining magazine and flipped it open without bothering to act nonchalant. While most of the coverage highlighted Abraham Danforth's political intentions, a number of interesting and potentially incriminating photographs were included as dirt on one of America's first families. Among them was a full-size picture of Heather wrapped in Toby's arms. Apparently he had been mistaken about destroying the only pictures of the kiss they had shared in Savannah. Another more surreptitious reporter had a captured a different angle from a spot he'd staked out earlier. An uncomfortable two-and-a-half-hour wait straddling a branch in a nearby tree ultimately earned the reporter a handsome commission from the tabloid. And Heather's undying disgust.

The caption proved as titillating as the picture. It insinuated that Toby Danforth hired a nanny to work with his "emotionally disturbed" son, more for physical attributes that were far more suitable for his bedroom than Dylan's nursery. Heather's face burned with shame. She glanced up to see every other patron in the establishment turn away in sudden preoccupation with their food or lack thereof.

Heather wished she didn't care a whit about what they thought. She knew she shouldn't.

Still, as a sensitive spirit, she was easily wounded. A wave of nausea washed over her as the coffee in her stomach soured. She gripped the edge of the table to keep her hands from shaking. Whether it was true or not, she had the definite feeling that everyone was laughing and pointing behind her back. The back of her neck grew hot and prickly.

When Josef humiliated her, she turned away from music to seek a new identity for herself. One that had given her a joyous beginning and faith in her own ability to shape her future. Unfortunately, she didn't know how to outrun the innuendo of a nationally syndicated publication, albeit one of dubious repute. Her parents, already disappointed in her, were sure to completely disown her now.

And what about Dylan? Heather knew how cruel children could be. There was no telling how his mother might react to such ugly publicity. Would she use it as ammunition in court to gain full custody of her son?

In her heart, Heather knew that falling in love with Toby had been a terrible, wonderful mistake. She simply hadn't counted on such a personal mistake being magnified and vilified in the press.

Dylan pushed his bowl away and swiped at the chocolate dribbling down his chin with the back of his arm, indicating he was ready to go.

Heather had to clear the lump from her throat before asking him, "Have you had enough?"

Nodding his head yes, the child looked perplexed by the tears shimmering in her eyes.

"Me, too," she said, meaning much more than he could possibly understand.

Heather paid their bill without saying another word and pretended not to hear the grizzled old man at the counter elbow his companion in the side.

"Think the little lady'd consider being my bed warmer—er, I mean nanny, Charlie?"

"Dunno, but I'd sure like a tonsillectomy like the one she gave her boss...."

Their words echoed in her ears as Heather stepped from the air-conditioned building into the bright light of day. The worst thing about falling in love with Toby was that her previous numbness had finally worn off, leaving her all the more vulnerable to the searing pain that engulfed her and left her feeling so all alone. If the highs with Toby were breathtaking, the lows were enough to suck the breath right out of her. Heather ached all over.

For once she was grateful for Dylan's silence. At least she didn't have to worry that he would tell his father about the many tears she'd shed on the long road home.

"I'm giving you my two weeks' notice."

Heather's words reverberated off the walls of the Double D and ricocheted inside Toby's brain like a bullet gone wild. Dylan was napping and the house was so still that every sound was amplified. The antique cuckoo clock in the kitchen alerted the house that it was three o'clock. The dishwasher clicked into its rinse cycle. And Toby felt the world shift beneath his feet.

He couldn't fathom what could have possibly occurred between the time he'd kissed Heather goodbye in the morning and now to make her say such a thing. A million thoughts raced through his head, most centering on what he could have possibly done to upset her. Picking one of the many excuses Sheila used to divorce him, he asked Heather if she simply found the town too rustic for her tastes. His attempt at flippancy fell as flat as his heart.

"No, too cosmopolitan actually," Heather replied, handing over the tabloid with shaking hands.

Toby scanned the article before hurling the magazine across the room in disgust.

"Is that what this is all about?" he demanded to

know. "I can't believe you'd let this piece of trash bother you."

"Maybe I didn't grow up with it the way you did. And maybe I'm more concerned about how this might affect you and Dylan than how it affects me personally."

"And maybe you're just looking for an excuse to run away."

Heather flinched, and he realized that he must have struck a nerve. He reached out a hand and brushed it against the side of her face. She took a deep breath and rested her cheek in the palm of his hand for a second. For eternity. With the pad of his thumb, Toby wiped away the tear that rolled down her face.

"What are you afraid of, sweetheart?"

"Of embarrassing you," Heather admitted. "Of compromising the progress Dylan's made for my own selfish desires."

Toby's laugh was almost a bark. "You could never embarrass me, and by the time Dylan will be able to read this, I'd like to think he'd have more discriminating tastes than to let something so base bother him. I certainly don't."

Heather pushed his hand away and swallowed against the tightening of her throat. "You can joke about it all you want, but the truth of the matter is it won't be long before Dylan will be old enough to question our relationship. A relationship stuck in neutral because neither one of us wants to commit to more than the physical. I can't see myself as your lover indefinitely, and I don't want to play the kind of games that require me to withhold love as a way to force you into marriage.''

She held up her hand to stop Toby from interrupting her.

"Look. I've studied this from every angle, and the only thing that makes sense is for me to go back to school this fall and work on my teaching certification. That way everyone can save face, and we can part as friends.''

As she continued babbling on about her plans to obtain a student loan and register for classes early, Toby looked at her as if she were asking to be helped into a straitjacket. While it was true that he had become somewhat inured to unwelcome publicity very early on in his life, he couldn't believe that Heather would actually let something as inconsequential as the *National Tattler* come between them. He wondered if her hypersensitivity was rooted in a painful past, or if she was simply mortified thinking of her parents and friends seeing her in such a compromising photograph splashed across the page of such a scandalous rag.

Toby never claimed to understand the complexities of the female mind. His ex lived to see her picture in the press, all too often lamenting Toby's aversion to the kind of elite social events that attracted the media. She mistakenly assumed fame under any circumstance was a good thing. Knowing

Sheila, she'd be pea-green with envy at the very picture causing Heather such grief. As much as Toby preferred Heather's attitude toward tabloid journalism, given the circumstances, he wished she could see it for what it was worth—little more than the paper on which it was printed.

Toby experienced a terrible sense of déjà vu as he recalled the day that Sheila announced she was leaving him. He had been secretly relieved to end the charade of their marriage. When Heather said those same words, he was rendered completely incapacitated. It would be far easier to lose a limb than to lose the gentle soul who had infused his life with hope and love. Feeling sucker-punched, he knew he had to do something drastic to get her to stay. Somehow he had to fix things between them. He had to make her understand that tawdry words had no power to tarnish a love as rare as theirs. Heather was no more the gold-digging tramp the press made her out to be than he was the playboy that they wanted so desperately to portray him as.

The solution came to Toby so easily that he knew in an instant it was what he wanted all along—a reason to put aside old fears and make a forever commitment to their relationship. A way for Heather to save face. A way to keep his child's best interest at heart. A way to proclaim his love to the entire world. A way to make things right.

Without any further ado, he knelt down in front of Heather and took both her hands into his. He stared into her eyes as if searching the starry sky for answers to the universe. A universe he longed to share with her for eternity.

"Miss Heather Burroughs," he began, slipping into the distinctly lyrical pattern of speech with which he'd been raised. "Would you do me the honor of marrying me?"

Twelve

Heather looked at Toby in disbelief. Here he was on his knees asking her to marry him and he hadn't ever so much as told her that he loved her. She could think of only one reason for him to propose out of the clear blue like this. From his reaction to the article she had shown him, it had nothing to do with salvaging his family name. And everything to do with her decision to tender her resignation.

She should have known that concern for Dylan would supersede everything else in Toby's life. As much as she admired him for that, her heart would not let her accept the offer that her head told her only an idiot would refuse. Toby Danforth was handsome, rich and compassionate. He was a good friend, a great father and an even better lover. Nonetheless, Heather had come a long way in terms of demanding self-respect since the day she broke away from those who would manipulate her talents to their own ends. As much as she loved Dylan, she didn't believe that was reason enough to marry his father.

"I can't marry you just so you don't have to look for another nanny," she said softly.

Clenched inside the velvet gloves of her words were granite fists. Toby drew back as if he had actually been struck, then reached up to tenderly stroke her cheek with the back of one hand.

"Sweetheart, whatever gave you that idea?"

Heather's face tingled where he touched her. Still, she could hardly compromise her future for an endearment that could melt the polar ice cap. Weariness weighed down her reasoning.

"If nothing else, your timing."

A note of exasperation crept into Toby's voice. "I thought this was what you wanted. Why else would you throw that rag of a magazine in my face if not to make me feel obliged to make an honest woman of you and prove something to the rest of the world?"

Heather stiffened under the accusation. Ugly words hurt, but now that the truth was out in the open she had no choice but to deal with it. Clearly, Toby felt she was manipulating him in much the same way she felt he was willing to use her just to make his life easier. In the same way her parents and Josef used her to promote their own aspirations. She'd vowed never to let anyone claim her life for their personal goals again. She believed that she deserved to be loved as a woman first, and a mother second.

"Those aren't exactly the words a girl hopes to hear when a man proposes," she told him flatly.

"I never said I was any good with words."

Toby's voice climbed with his frustration. "And I imagine that even if I found the right ones now, they'd be suspect in your mind. Wouldn't they?"

Heather shook her head sadly. "Probably."

She was as taken aback by Toby's sudden anger as by the fact that, even under duress, he seemed unable to utter the three little words that were the foundation of all good marriages. She had to wonder if he even knew what they were. Having heard him profess his love openly to his son on numerous occasions, she was inclined to believe that was not the case. Toby simply wasn't in love with her.

Oh, she was good enough to be a mother to his son, good enough to warm his bed at night, good enough to marry out of convenience, but she did not lay claim to his heart—and suspected she never would. Heather supposed she should thank him for being honest with her rather than leading her on like Josef had, but at the moment it was everything she could do to keep her composure in front of him.

Inside she was falling apart.

"I'm sorry," she said plainly enough.

Her refusal stung. Pride kept Toby from begging. He was sorry that he ruined the moment with his inability to express what was in his heart. It wasn't exactly like he had a lot of experience in proposing. He'd never asked anyone to marry him before. Sheila had popped the question herself on the heels of announcing that she was pregnant with his child. Being of honorable character, he had simply gone along with her wishes and done the right thing. And although his brief marriage had brought him little happiness, because it had given him a wonderful son, he could not bring himself to regret it. He could not imagine what Heather's leaving would do to him, let alone Dylan.

Toby got off his knees and put his weight squarely back onto the same two feet that had carried him this far into life with his backbone, if not his heart, intact.

"I'm sorry, too. Sorry that I don't have the right words for you. It's obvious where my son gets his inability to communicate."

Heather held up her hands to stop him. She gestured toward the open doorway. "That doesn't affect his hearing any."

Dylan was standing there, clutching his favorite blanket and looking at them with a worried expression on his face. Though unable to verbalize his thoughts, he was clearly upset to hear the two most important people in his life raising their voices to one another. Heather rushed to his side and bent down to wipe away the single tear that rolled down his cheek.

Taking him in her arms, she hastened to assure him. "Everything's going to be fine."

"Don't lie to the boy," Toby barked. "His mother told him that just before she left for good. Until you showed up, the last word he ever said was goodbye."

He extended a hand to his son. Dylan looked to Heather. Unable to utter a single word herself, she simply nodded her approval and gave him over to his father without a fight. She didn't know what she could possibly say to make Toby stay and work out their problems, what she could possibly say to make him love her as much as she loved him.

"Come on, son. Let's get out of here before I say something I'll regret."

The door swung shut behind them with a bang that reverberated throughout the house. The immediate silence and a feeling of being completely alone again engulfed Heather. She put her head in her hands and sobbed without making a sound. How ironic, she thought, that she had come here to help Dylan find his voice and lost hers in the process.

An hour passed without any sign of the two men in her life. She imagined they had gone into town, leaving her to her own devices. Evening cast a long shadow over the gleaming piano in the center of the room. Having no other way to express herself without fear of further repercussions, Heather turned to the one friend who had never abandoned her—even in the dark days when she deliberately turned her back on it. Approaching the piano with a sense of trepidation, she hoped her hands remembered their training.

Nimble fingers gave voice to her angst. The song she played in the fading light was moving in the depth of emotion it conveyed. Echoing off the walls, the highs and lows of those notes resounded off mountain walls that sheltered them from the outside world. A world that did not understand the complexity of a woman's heart.

How good it felt to let the music speak for her. Heather was bent over the piano keys, immersed in a heartbreaking melody, attempting to loosen the pain deep inside of her, when Dylan appeared out of nowhere. Scratched and bloody, he tugged at her sleeve to get her attention and struggled to convey a message of grave importance.

"What's wrong?" she asked, jolted from her trancelike state by his appearance.

He opened his mouth, but no sound came out. Grabbing him by the shoulders, Heather implored, "Please, Dylan, tell me what's happened."

Tears pooled in eyes the exact shade as his father's. Squeezing them shut, he concentrated hard and opened his mouth again.

"D-d-d…D-d-daddy…hurt…"

Fear swallowed Heather whole. She was off the piano bench in an instant and racing toward the front door. Her feet never hit the floor. Dylan was right behind her. Not knowing which way to go, Heather stopped only long enough to scoop the frightened toddler into her arms.

"Where's Daddy?"

Dylan pointed with a dirty finger. Heather spied a tractor in the back pasture. Her heart stopped beating. All too often, ranch accidents proved fatal. Praying she didn't twist an ankle, Heather sprinted across freshly tilled soil with Dylan on her hip. The roar in her ears drummed out all other sounds, even the screaming of her own voice as she called Toby's name again and again.

As she closed in upon the scene, Heather saw that the tractor was overturned. She might have known Toby would take his frustrations out on big machinery, trying to score a drought-hardened earth he found softer than her own hard heart! What she would give to replay the incident that drove him to fate's destructive path.

Looking like a fallen dinosaur, the tractor was still running on its side. Going nowhere, one wheel spun uselessly in the air. Even if Toby were able to respond to her frantic calls, Heather knew it would be impossible to discern his voice over the roar of machinery. Setting Dylan on the ground, she prayed the man she loved was not pinned beneath the immovable mountain of metal. When the tractor had toppled and Toby realized there was nothing he could do to prevent it, she imagined his first thoughts were for his son. In her mind's eye, Heather could see him throwing Dylan clear before giving thought to his own safety.

Thunder boomed in the distance.

Heather circled the tractor and found Toby's lifeless form next to it. His blood stained the long prairie grass and seeped into the parched earth. One arm was bent beneath his twisted body. He had fallen on the side of the field that he had just plowed, somewhat cushioning his fall. Dropping to her knees beside him, she sobbed and pressed her head to his heart. The faint sound of its beating kindled hope in her breast.

Checking his pulse, she imagined minuscule pressure in return when she squeezed his hand. Her lips upon his caused his eyelids to flutter open briefly. She bathed his bloody face with her tears.

Dialing 911 was of little use in this situation. By the time an ambulance arrived, Toby could well bleed to death. Heather looked to the gathering storm clouds and tore back across the open field. Promising to be back in a minute, she told Dylan to stay put. Their only hope was to get Toby to the emergency room as quickly as possible.

Out of breath by the time she reached his pickup, she silently thanked him for always leaving his keys in the ignition. Snakebites, grizzly maulings and un-

foreseen accidents were far more likely than theft in
such a remote region. The only crime that concerned
Heather at the moment was the possibility of Toby
dying without her ever telling him she loved him.

A few scattered raindrops splattered against the
windshield as Heather started up the one-ton pickup.
Any other day she would be grateful for the moisture. Today she could scarcely afford to run the risk
of getting mired in the mud. Swearing, she turned
the vehicle toward the scene of the accident and
lurched forward, mindless of nothing but getting to
Toby as quickly as possible. She threw the vehicle
into four-wheel drive and fastened her seat belt on
the fly. Had she not, it was likely she would have
knocked herself out by hitting her head on the roof
as she raced across the rough plowed field.

Dylan was crying next to his father when Heather
pulled up beside them. She parked the pickup as
close as she possibly could without endangering either of them. She didn't have enough adrenaline to
lift an entire tractor off a man, but there was enough
of that life preserver flowing in her bloodstream to
manage to hoist a 175-pound man into the cab of a
pickup. It wasn't until she tried getting Toby to his
feet that she realized how grotesquely disfigured his
arm was. Try as she might to be gentle, it was all
she could do to fold him into the front seat. He
groaned before slipping back into unconsciousness,
his arm flopping uselessly at his side.

Heather tossed Dylan into the truck beside her and

told him to hold his father's head in his lap. It seldom rained in Wyoming, but when it did it usually arrived in a torrent, flooding gullies and washing away precious topsoil. If she could make it out of the field before it turned to clay, Heather figured there was a good chance they wouldn't get stuck.

Her wheels spun. Every minute counted, but she didn't want to bury the pickup by gunning it in her haste. She pressed down on the accelerator slowly and eased her way toward the gravel road. The only thing separating her from that road was a nasty-looking barbed wire fence. It stood no chance against her will and seven thousand pounds of Ford-tough truck hurtling toward it in the rain.

Like the pop of a starting gun, the twang of barbed wire signaled Heather's hope of making it to the hospital in record time. Gravel churned in all directions as they hit the county road. Just about that time, the hail started. The size of marbles, the hailstones plinked off the roof and the hood of Toby's new vehicle, rippling it with dents. Considering the new barb wire bra across the front of the truck, Heather doubted the insurance company would quarrel over the cost of such mundane repairs.

Once they reached the main highway, she placed that 911 call on the cell phone that was considered standard equipment on most Wyoming trucks, and alerted the hospital to expect them shortly. She flipped on her emergency flashers. The road was slick, and she took care not to hydroplane at high speeds. The last thing she wanted to do was cause yet another accident in her haste to save a life. All the way into town, Dylan petted his father's head and cooed reassuringly into his ear.

Without taking her eyes off the road, Heather told him, ''You're a real hero.''

In light of his own traumatic experience on that tractor, Dylan's speaking in order to save his father was nothing short of a miracle. Heather always believed that the boy would talk when he was ready. She just hadn't counted on a life-and-death situation proving her right. Nor had she realized just how important it was to speak from the heart while there was still time for those precious words to be heard. If God would but spare Toby's life, Heather vowed to never again let pride get in the way of love's true course.

''I love you. I love you. I love you,'' she repeated over and over to the rhythm of the hail and the swish of windshield wipers.

''Looks pretty bad. We may have to amputate.''

The emergency room nurse was not aware that Toby was conscious when she uttered that dire prediction. Even if she was, she would have sworn that the shot she administered immediately thereafter would make him forget anything he heard while she was prepping him anyway. She was wrong.

Because his son needed him and because he was a fighter, Toby Danforth hung on to those words through a fog of pain as he clung to life itself. Tenaciously.

When he came to, hours later, he was surprised to see Heather asleep in the chair next to his bed. Her neck was bent at an uncomfortable angle causing her hair to spill over her shoulder in a waterfall of gold. Dark circles rimmed her closed eyes. Toby longed to reach out and touch this delicate creature just once more, but his strength failed him. It hurt to think that any chance they may have had for a future together was as shattered as the arm he heard crack just before he passed out.

Wrapped tightly in blankets and as yet unable to move, he couldn't tell whether that arm was still attached to his body beneath his hospital garb. The nurse's remark about amputation echoed in his ears. If Heather hadn't wanted him when he proposed to her before the accident, he couldn't imagine asking her to accept him as less than a whole man—without two strong arms to hold and protect her.

As if the incredible woman who rescued him needed his protection. Thinking it unfair to ask her to marry him given the reclusive nature of his life and his son's special needs, he wouldn't expect Heather to sign away her youth and vitality to a cripple. The sight of her stirring in a shaft of light filtering in through the window touched all of his senses at once. Her eyelids opened to reveal a pair of dove-gray eyes that softened the instant she saw him.

"God, but you're beautiful," he mumbled.

Toby wasn't sure why that would cause her to burst into tears, but she did. Smothering him with kisses, she told him just how happy she was that he was alive. He wasn't so sure about that. Once Heather left for good, his life wouldn't be worth much to anyone—except to a sensitive little boy who needed him to be both his mother and father. And the parents who would likely expect Toby to move home so they could treat him like an invalid for the rest of his life.

Heather tucked a strand of hair behind one ear and stepped back to stare at him earnestly. Having an epiphany on the long, perilous ride to town, she was ready to bare her soul.

"If it's okay with you, I'd like to reconsider that proposal you made earlier today."

The jump in Toby's heart rate registered on the monitor next to his bed.

"You think you could do a better job, I suppose," he said. His voice, though weak, reflected an amusement that his eyes did not share.

Giving him a lopsided smile, Heather knelt beside his bed in a classic proposal position. "I love you."

As much as Toby needed to stop her from making a fool of them both, those words filled him with such a sense of joy that he wanted more than anything else in this world to believe his ears.

"Ssshhh…" he whispered. "You don't have to—"

"Don't shush me. God and I had a nice, long talk on the way to getting you here, and we decided that you need me. Not just Dylan, big boy, but you. It seems I need you, too. I'm willing to work at marriage on whatever terms you think fair. If you'll just give me a chance, I think I can make you learn to love me."

Toby choked on the fist that was stuck in his throat. "Learn—to love you?" he stammered. For a woman who said she wanted romance in a marriage proposal, she certainly made hers sound more like a business proposition than a matter of the heart. A man who believed in proving himself not by words but by actions, he couldn't fathom that she didn't know how out-of-his-mind crazy in love with her he was.

Was it possible she truly believed he proposed to her simply because she was good with Dylan? Was she really so thick that she believed he would make a lifetime commitment based on anything other than his feelings for her? Didn't she know that the kind of earth-moving passion they shared was something so special that poets couldn't find words to describe it adequately?

He was such an idiot! When she rejected his proposal out of hand, he had reacted like some hot-headed kid, rushing off without getting to the heart of the matter. Attempting to assuage his wounded pride by getting behind the wheel of a monstrous tractor and running it into the ground wasn't the smartest move he'd ever made, either. Luckily for him, Heather was made of sterner stuff. If not for her cool head, he could well have died within walking distance of his house.

He berated himself for not staying to work things out when she first called his motives into question. Now it was much too late for mending fences or limbs.

"My arm—" he began.

"What about it?"

That she looked so genuinely surprised he would mention it made Toby ache for opportunities lost.

"I can't expect you to marry half a man."

"Tobias Danforth!" Heather exclaimed. "I can't believe you think I'm so shallow that I care more about how you look than what's inside you."

She, too, had heard the hospital buzz that his arm might be amputated, but refused to believe it until she heard it straight from the doctor's mouth. Even then, Toby's parents, who she called immediately after admitting him, assured her that they wanted a specialist to look at their son before any such drastic measure be taken. Having booked a private jet, Harold and Miranda were due to arrive any moment to lend their support and help their son and grandson any way they could. Heather envied Toby their limitless love—and longed to share it with him.

"Whether you have one arm or three makes no difference to me. I love you. Not your arm or your pocketbook or your family name or some stupid, strong-and-silent cowboy stereotype that you'd let ruin your life if it weren't for me. Understand this— nothing is going to change my feelings for you. Nothing. I love you, and I love your son. It's that simple. Let's not make it any more difficult than that."

"I love you, too."

Seeing the tears spill down her cheeks at the admission, Toby rebuked himself for not saying those words long ago. They had the power to make him feel whole.

Even though he wasn't.

No matter what he wanted for himself, Toby could not in good conscience let such a young, vibrant woman throw her life away without giving serious consideration to what it would be like to be married to a man who would need help simply getting dressed every morning. On more than one occasion, Heather had told him his disposition was less than sweet on his good days. He imagined he would be a bear to live with as he learned to function without an appendage. It wouldn't be right to hold her to a declaration of love made under the duress of such a terrible accident. He didn't want her to make a commitment to him out of a sense of pity.

Again Toby tried to explain. "I love you and I'd ask you to marry me again, but my arm—"

"Is full of pins, and you won't be doing any manual labor for a while. But don't worry. A little mend-

ing and a lot therapy and you should regain full use
of it in time for the fall stock show.''

The doctor who stepped into the room was young
and cocky. The fact that he happened to be wearing
cowboy boots and was the bearer of tremendous
news excused his high-flying bedside manner. Toby
closed his eyes and exhaled the accumulated fear
from his lungs as the surgeon continued with his
prognosis.

''You also have a bad concussion, which must
explain why I thought I heard you talking about
marriage when I walked in the room. The Toby Danforth I know vowed he would never get married
again, and made me promise to knock some sense
into his head if he ever so much as mentioned it.''

Toby's smile lit up the entire hospital wing.
''That won't be necessary. I knocked some sense
into my own head the hard way.''

He turned his attention away from the doctor and
focused his entire being on Heather. ''Like I was
saying, I love you. And I want to marry you. For
all the right reasons.''

The glow on Heather's face erased all doubts
Toby might have had. She wasn't the kind of
woman who needed roses and exotic settings and
romantic music in the background to accept a man's
heartfelt proposal. She just needed to hear the right
words. He thanked God that he had found them in
time to turn his life around. A future brimming with

promise need not be overshadowed by the mistakes of the past.

"I'd be honored to be your wife."

There was no false fluttering of eyelashes or Southern belle pretense in Heather's words. Just joyful acceptance. And a shimmer of passion glowing in her eyes.

Doc Cameron cleared his throat. Truth be told, he was jealous as could be. And a little uncomfortable being present at such a private moment. "I'd shake your hand if it weren't busted all to hell. What d'ya say I leave you two lovebirds alone to set a date?"

"If it were up to me, I'd have the minister who arrived to give me last rites marry us before he leaves the building. Barring that, you can expect an invitation any day," Toby informed him.

"I wouldn't miss it for the world," the doctor said. With that, he took his leave, promising to return momentarily with Dylan.

Toby felt his heart swell as he looked at his lovely wife-to-be. Moved by her courage and beauty, he couldn't help but ask, "Are you sure you're not the one with the concussion?"

"As positive as I am that I intend to take advantage of you all wrapped up tight in your blanket, helpless to resist my advances."

"Good thing I didn't crush that part of my anatomy," Toby whispered, glancing down at the prominent protrusion beneath his hospital covers.

Heather simultaneously blushed, laughed and

agreed with him as he proceeded to let her know he was already well on the road to recuperation. Despite his weakened state, Toby managed to free his good arm from under the covers. He wrapped that arm around her waist and dragged her close. Leaning over his bed, Heather kissed him tenderly, as if afraid of hurting him further. Toby would have none of it. He parted her lips with his tongue and intensified that kiss. When Heather made a move to draw away, he nuzzled the swell of her breasts straining against the buttons of her shirt and refused to let her go. She could scarcely breathe for the tightness surrounding her heart. Her knees grew so weak that she had to support herself by leaning a hand against his thigh.

"I do believe there's just enough room in this narrow little bed for two people if they were of a mind to consummate their upcoming wedding vows," Toby told her with glint in his eyes.

"Behave yourself," Heather warned as Dylan skipped into the room, clutching the hand of a cute high school candy striper who dropped him off at the door.

She had to restrain the boy from climbing up on the bed and accidentally injuring his father in his haste to give him a hug. He stood next to the bed as proud as could be and asked, "I did good, huh, Dad?"

Toby's eyes widened. The expression on his face said it all. He looked to Heather for confirmation that he wasn't imagining things. Running a hand through Dylan's unruly hair, she nodded her head.

"Your son saved your life. He was the one who came and got me. He *told* me you were hurt and led me to your side."

"He *told* you?" Toby repeated in disbelief. Was it possible God was so generous that He would grant a man more than one miracle a day?

"And, according to the nurses, he's been bragging to everyone in the hospital about what a big hero he is."

It took a moment for her words to sink into Toby's fractured skull. When they finally did, he almost jumped out of bed, forgetting that he wasn't up to a doing a jig just yet. Heather accommodated him by lifting Dylan up and setting him on the edge of the bed so they could share a group hug. That joyful embrace marked the beginning of their life as a family together.

A life that gave voice to all of their dreams.

* * * * *

Be sure to look for the next title in
DYNASTIES: THE DANFORTHS
with Sheri Whitefeather's
STEAMY SAVANNAH NIGHTS,
on sale in August.